Maddie & Sayara

By Sanjyot P. Dunung

Full Circle Media, Inc.
New York

Maddie & Sayara
Copyright © 2017 by Sanjyot P. Dunung

Published by Full Circle Media, Inc.
41 West 25th Street, New York, NY 10010 USA
For more information on bulk sales, please contact info@fcmediainc.com
For general information on this and other publications, please contact info@fcmediainc.com

www.maddieandsayara.com

ISBN: 978-1-943967-88-9 (Print Paperback)
ISBN: 978-1-943967-89-6 (eBook)

Cover by Chris Schmelter

First Edition 2017
10 9 8 7 6 5 4 3 2 1

Library of Congress Control Number: 2017952675

To all young people, whether in age or in spirit,
hoping to make the world better.

Maddie & Sayara

"We are birds in a gilded cage, Maddie," Sayara reflected. I could hear tears in her voice. "We may have all the treasures of the world, but we do not have the ones most valuable—freedom, equality, and respect. Those you have in abundance, Maddie. You are very lucky to have been born where you were. We have totally different lives just because I was born in the kingdom." Sayara tearfully whispered into the phone, "We're not so different, Maddie—you and me—so why does my world consider me so much less worthy than your world considers you? Why am I considered a burden, and you get to be a blessing?" Well, it wasn't so much a question, because I had no answer. I had no clue; neither of us did. But we both knew it to be our reality.

Maddie & Sayara tells the tale of two girls who find that their lives go down different paths just because of where they were born. Join them on their adventure as they challenge unfair rules and try to escape from dangerous and powerful forces.

.

Maddie & Sayara

By Sanjyot P. Dunung

Chapter 1

I first met Sayara in the Bahamas when we were both thirteen. We had been sent there to "vacation" by parents involved in their own busy lives. Vacation was my mom's way of getting personal time for herself, although Dad always joked that every day was her personal time as she didn't really do anything. Sayara and I were both there with our nannies, who were really our mothers-in-spirit. Not only that, but Sayara wanted to be an only child just like I did, since we each had an annoying younger brother. Well, I don't always want to be an only child, but don't tell Jason that. He still annoys me sometimes, but not as much as he did back then.

That day, I was floating along in the lazy river pool. I was peacefully content staring at the little bugs in the water flowing alongside my inner tube. I wondered about the tiny bugs—did the river feel like the ocean to them? I don't really mind bugs; reptiles are my only intense fear, but that's another story. My sunglasses kept getting splattered by the occasional spurt of water as I rounded bends. It was mellow, I was chill, and all was okay until I glanced to the side and saw a girl about my age sitting all princess-like on a sun chair, covered with a white towel. Was she cold? Who sits in the hot sun under a towel? And then I felt her eyes laser in on me—more like on my head—and my head of hair.

Why is that girl so rudely staring at me? I wondered. Hasn't she ever seen red hair? I hate it when my hair gets extra light from the sun—it becomes almost orange! Everyone looks at me like I'm a freak clown. Aunt AK always tells me that it's my oh-so-distinguishing feature and I will come to love it. Maybe someday. My mom always rubs it in with that sugary-sweet sarcastic voice, pretending that her suggestion is for my benefit, when it's really about her preferences: "Why don't you dye your hair a pretty chestnut brown like mine or Angie's?"

My older sister Angie has always gotten all the praise. You just know when you're not the favorite child. And with Mom and Angie, I've known that since I was a baby. Angie's "so pretty, so graceful, so smart ... all the boys like her." Whatever. My mom has always loved her so much better, probably just because she looks like my mom and acts like her, too. Mini-mom.

I used to wish that Aunt AK was my mom ... well, I guess that would have been pretty creepy since she's my dad's sister. But still. Adrienne Kate's her real name, but everyone calls her AK. She's always been so much nicer to me. She loves me as I am—wild red hair, goofy freckles, skinny legs too long for my growing body, and all. I've always wanted to be like her. She's not only pretty on the outside, but really kind on the inside. She always tells me that "the insides of a person are the only thing that matters," especially when I get frustrated that my body has grown taller than the rest of me has developed. I look like a boring matchstick, tall with no shape and a mop of red hair! I hate it, but I trust her and try to believe that she's right ... insides, insides, insides. That's what I tell myself. It sounds really sappy and corny, but what do I have to lose? Besides, she's so much fun. I can tell her anything, and she loves to play basketball and go on the fastest roller coasters like me.

Mom has always said it would be terrible if I grow up to be a loud tomboy like AK. Okay, so Aunt AK does have a really loud, weird laugh. But she loves me as is, and I have come to now realize in my brief years of life how much that really means.

Aunt AK used to hang around with me even more a few years ago after she sold her real business, something about helping companies hire people. Whatever, something like that. Anyhow, she made a gazillion dollars when she sold it. She now has a jewelry business and gets to wear jeans to work and travel to really cool places like Iceland whenever she wants. That's what I want, to be Aunt AK when I grow up … okay, maybe without the weird, loud laugh.

That day in the Bahamas, I really wished Aunt AK had come on vacation with us. I remember thinking that Aunt AK would at least hang out with me and not spend the week at a spa and yoga retreat.

All my mom ever does is nap, and when she's awake, she's usually in her "silent meditation mood," the "don't bother me" kind. Or she goes to the spa, plays tennis, or, worst of all, nags me about what to do or how to look. All my mom wants me to be is a nice, pretty girl who marries a nice, rich boy. Lame and totally outdated. I don't even have a boyfriend! Geez. And my mom is worried that I'll never be able to get a husband. Maybe that's why she obsesses about my freakish hair.

On that day when I first saw Sayara, I remember thinking that her jet-black hair was really pretty and my mom would definitely like it. She also looked delicate and dainty, just like my mom keeps wishing I would be.

But she wouldn't stop staring at me.

I just wanted to chill and read—alone. I loved the lazy river ride, although it wasn't really a ride since all you did was float. Why did they even call it a ride? Why not just call it a lazy river float? The name made me giggle as it did sound funny, even if it was true. Luckily most everyone was somewhere else in the resort. The river was almost empty except for Jason, my annoying kid brother, and me.

Linda, our nanny, was half asleep on her pool chair. We didn't need to be watched constantly anymore so she could relax. Linda's taken care of me since I was born and feels more like my real mom than just the nanny. What makes a mom, anyhow? Just 'cause she birthed me? As my mother likes to always remind me, I don't think that makes her a real mom. What about really loving and caring for your kids and spending fun time with them? Shouldn't that count for more? And truth be told, Aunt AK and Linda take much more care of us than our birth mom. Can I call her that? My birth mom? Makes me sound adopted, doesn't it? Well, I wish that Aunt AK would adopt me! But my dad. I love my dad and he loves me as is. I guess it's a package deal—for now.

Linda has way more patience than me, especially with my mom. I get so mad at Mom and Linda tells me, "It's okay, Maddie-girl, just be brushin' it off." Linda's cool. She thinks Mom is mean too, but she's just really polite to her because she has to be. Mom's her boss. And Jason—well, Mom doesn't really pay any attention to him. She says he's "his father's son" and his father's responsibility. If he weren't my brother, I'd feel sorry for him for being neglected by Mom. But at least Jason has Dad, Linda, and me. Angie is too focused on herself to think about anyone else. And when she started university, she became way too cool for any of us.

That girl, she was still staring. Time to tell her off.

"Hey, you—" I called out.

But a giant splash interrupted me. "Jason! You're a jerk!" I know I was in the water already, but the brat made me wetter and drenched my book.

Quit grinning, Jason.

"You're a freak, Maddie! Your hair was on 'fire' so I had to put it out." He made that stupid face that he always does and rolled his eyes. "Freak, freak."

"Shut up." I really hate it when he calls me a freak because of my red hair. I know I'm not supposed to let it bother me, but it does. "You're an idiot." Oh, why did I have to have a nine-year-old brother? Why, oh why? A puppy would have been so much better!

"Freak, freak, freak," he chanted as he ran from the flowing river back to the big pool where he had been playing Nerf pool volleyball with a bunch of other boys.

"I don't think you're a freak," said a calm, soft voice. Who said that? I looked up to see that girl with the staring big brown eyes looking at me.

"Thanks, but my brother is a jerk, and I hate my hair. My mom wants me to color it, and my brother hears her nagging me," I told her.

"I like your red hair. It must be nice to have something different from everyone else. I'm tired of my black hair. Everyone at home has black hair," the girl informed me. "Actually, yours isn't quite red, it's kind of red-brown-blond. It's a mix of colors."

"Yeah, it's a mix of shades, 'mutt hair' as my mom calls it. My mom says it was all a pretty shade of blond when I was born, but somehow I messed it all up like I do everything and now it's this weird mix. She can't wait to get me to color it all blond or brown, but I don't want to. Seems like it wouldn't be me then," I told her defiantly. In truth, it wasn't just my hair that was mutt-like. It was me, too. I didn't fit neatly into one category. I wasn't completely a girly girl. I wasn't completely a tomboy, either. I was a little bit of both. I wasn't completely an athlete or a nerd, maybe halfway in between. I certainly wasn't one of the cool girls and definitely not a mean girl, either. At least I hoped not. Why did everyone want you to be one label or another? I saw myself as a little bit of everything, all mixed together. I was a girl, plus I loved sports and being strong. I loved fixing things. I was smart at school, but I loved vacation, too. I had a few really good friends, both girls and boys. Mila and Mikey were my besties, but I also liked hanging out with some people in my family, like my dad and Aunt AK. I was a mix of all shades, just like my hair.

"Well then, you should keep it just as it is, reddish brown. I like it—it's very charming," she informed me in a most serious, grown-up tone.

She was quick with her opinions, but kinder than my mom with them, too. Suddenly, I realized I liked this new hair coach of mine.

"Thanks, but my mom won't like that. She wants to make me look like a girl," I replied.

"What does that mean? You already look like a girl, don't you?" she snickered curiously.

"Not according to my mother!" I sighed. "She wants me to be all prim and proper and delicate." My face must have looked very contorted and frustrated because the new girl just burst out laughing.

"You're so funny, and you're not a freak! My name is Sayara." With that, she grabbed an inner tube and got into the lazy river next to me.

"My name is Maddie." This girl might be okay. She didn't think I was a freak like everyone else.

"How come everyone where you live has black hair?" I was curious. Everyone back home had all kinds of hair, different styles, colors, and shades—blond, brown, red, black, pink, purple, green. I had seen people dye their hair all sorts of colors.

"Pretty much everyone has the same black hair color in the kingdom where I live, all long and straight. It feels like a uniform sometimes. I want to cut mine really short, but my mom won't let me," my new hair coach Sayara told me. "My mom wants me to look like a girl too, just like your mom, I guess."

"Moms are funny that way. I'll be a different kind of mom when I grow up," I announced. I really hadn't thought about it much, but at that moment I suddenly realized that I didn't want to be like my mom.

"Wow, that's really bold to say, Maddie. At home, all respectful girls grow up the same way."

"Respectful? Respectful of what?" I was respectful … most of the time, I think.

Sayara smiled. "I mean that we must listen and obey our parents and family. It is expected of us." Drawn into what was in my hands, she changed the topic. "What are you reading? The pages got wet when your brother jumped on you."

"I know. Jason annoys me! But it's okay, they'll dry, and it's an old copy. *The Secret Garden*. I really love the older stories."

"I've never heard of it. Is it good?" she asked, only half interested.

"Totally. You can read mine if you want. I've read it before, and I saw the movie and the play. I love it—it's about a funky girl whose parents die in India, and she has to go live with her uncle in England in a creepy old house in the middle of nowhere. There are all these scary noises at night, but she doesn't listen to the house rules and stay in her room. And she finds her handicapped, spoiled cousin whining in a room 'cause he thinks he can't walk. The doctors and the housekeeper have all these rules to supposedly protect his health, but they really end up forcing him to be stuck in bed. But the girl tells him to stop being bratty and then secretly teaches him how to walk again in this really pretty secret garden in the back of the house. If she had listened to the housekeeper and doctors, her cousin would never have even walked! I hate when grown-ups tell you that you have to do something just because that's the way it's always been. I love that she secretly disobeys the rules, which are stupid to begin with."

"I know," noted Sayara, "I hear that all the time at home, too. My dad always says 'It's the way of our beliefs, so we must do the same.'" Her voice had deepened to mimic her father. "So what if the belief is wrong? I always tell him that a bunch of years ago, people used to believe the world was flat. Can you imagine some poor guy walking and walking, thinking he's going to fall off the edge of the earth, then just walking in a really big loop and coming back to where he started? Sometimes a belief is wrong. That's why I wanna be an astronaut, explore the unknowns and question what we think we know. Like, what if there really are UFOs? I hate when adults think they know it all and we kids don't. What's wrong with asking questions or wondering if there's something we don't know about science or life or whatever?"

"I so get it. My dad and Aunt AK are more chill, but my mom always expects me to obey her annoying rules even when they make no sense or are outdated by like a hundred years!"

The annoying rules piqued her interest. "Same here!" Sayara exclaimed with excitement. "There are so many rules at home and I secretly try to break them, but sometimes I get caught! Last week I was playing soccer with our watchman, and my mom saw me and I got in huge trouble."

"Really, you got in trouble for playing soccer?" I asked. Where did this girl live? Her rules suddenly seemed much sillier than the ones I was stuck with.

"Yeah, girls aren't allowed to play sports, especially not in public and with boys. But Rajiv, one of our watchmen, has been teaching me soccer since I was a little girl. I love playing soccer and I'm pretty good, or at least I think I am. But there's no team for me and no one to really play with. Even Rajiv told me that we have to be careful now that I'm growing up. Pretty soon, I won't even be able to talk to him without wearing a tent."

"What's that? You have to wear a tent, like in camping?" I know, I know. I was totally clueless.

"No, not like camping. But it's like a total body tent that covers all of you, even your face. I don't like it. When you're inside of it, no one can see your face, and I feel invisible. I can't run around in one, and I feel like I'm constantly tripping on the edges. I really don't want to wear it, but my mom says all respectful girls have to when they grow up."

"I don't have to wear one and I'm respectful … I think." Who makes all these rules? I wondered.

"I know, it doesn't seem fair. My cousin Themi hates to wear one too, and she tells everyone it's wrong to force girls and women. She says it should be a choice to wear one or not to wear one. Each person should be able to decide for herself. Themi is so cool and has so much courage. She tells me that one day, girls at home will be able to play soccer and will get to choose what they want to wear." Sayara had a smile on her face, but it was the kind of smile you make when you don't know what else to do. I didn't think it was a happy smile.

"Don't you get to decide if you want to wear it or not?"

"Nope, it doesn't work that way. If you want to keep honor with your family, you have to obey all these rules. There's no choice."

"That's not right. Linda, my nanny, always tells me that we have the freedom to make choices, good ones and dumb ones, but it's always our choice."

Speaking of Linda, I saw her waving me in from the pool-side. "Maddie, time for lunch."

"Hey, gotta go to lunch. Meet you back here later?" I liked this new girl even though she came from a place with really strict and weird rules.

"Sure, I have to go find my ayah, too."

"Text me when you're back." I climbed out of the pool and gave Sayara my number.

After lunch, Sayara and I decided to brave the Shark Dive waterslide, which whisked you down into a clear tunnel through a pool of sharks. It sounds scarier than it was! The sharks were the easy part—it was the almost vertical drop at the beginning that made us lose our stomachs, but it turned out that both Sayara and I loved the speed of waterslides and roller coasters. The drop on that waterslide was intense, and then to go through the clear tunnel with sharks swimming all around was so cool. It was my favorite part of the entire resort. Plus, the lines were short, and waiting in lines is such a drag. There was another clear tunnel slide that came through the same shark pool, but it was a gentle ride and all the little kids did it with their parents. I didn't mind the little kids—I sometimes babysat my neighbors at home—but that line took forever. So Sayara and I stayed on Shark Dive, which really made you feel like you were diving straight down into the shark tunnel.

"Let's go again, Maddie!" Sayara called out to me as we landed in the pool at the end of the Shark Dive for the fifth time. Our times were exactly the same. So we trudged to the top of the tower stairs. We both lay down in our tracks, our hands and elbows tucked in. The tighter we'd be, the faster we'd go.

"Let's be timing twins again, Maddie," Sayara insisted. She seemed to always want to be the same as me, which I kinda liked. She didn't care about beating me like Jason or Angie always had to. And, in so many ways, this new friend of mine and I were a lot alike. We loved the water and sports. Our days were filled with making sandcastles on the beach, learning to windsurf, and taming the wild water rides. Our evenings were spent hanging out in the teen room playing Ping-Pong. Even at that, we ended up tying, although when we played as doubles against some other kids, we always won.

Even though Sayara and I had just met, we felt like twins in spirit. We both loved to eat, and ice cream was our favorite.

We liked the same music—we even had the same songs in our playlist favorites! It was nice-weird how much we had in common. We swapped stories of our best friends and family at home, even our crushes. I told her about one of the guys on our middle-school basketball team, Andre, who was kinda cute and really good on the court. Sayara didn't see a lot of guys at her all-girls school, but she was infatuated with this actor I had never heard about. She was also very curious about my friendship with Mikey, one of my two best buddies since preschool. Sayara didn't really have boys as friends. She had a younger brother and cousins, but that was it. Sayara and I talked for hours and seemed to want the same things in life. We had so much in common. Twins, only from different moms.

Chapter 2

On the morning of the fourth day, I woke with an odd feeling in my stomach. I wasn't sure if I had eaten something funny the night before or if it was belly butterflies telling me something was up. I get those sometimes when something weird is going to happen. Aunt AK says it's my sixth sense, and I have to learn to trust it. When I went down to the breakfast café, I looked for Sayara to eat with as I had done all week.

I saw her breeze in but with a serious face. She was wearing jeans, not her bathing suit. What gives? I wondered.

"Maddie, I can't hang out anymore. We have to go home." Her breathless voice made me realize that this was serious.

"What happened? I thought you were here for the whole week, too?"

"My cousin Themi ... my cousin ..." Her voice stammered as she tried to continue. "Oh, Maddie." All week, she had talked about her cousin Themi a lot, sort of her big sister and best friend all rolled into one. Sayara's voice crackled in a whisper, "Themi has been arrested. It's terrible! And my dad wants us home immediately." Her eyes lowered both from sadness and concern.

"Oh my gosh. What did she do?" Arrested. I had NEVER known anyone who had been arrested.

"She was caught driving!" Sayara exclaimed.

"And?" Did she have a bad accident and hurt someone? I wondered.

"And, what?" Sayara questioned impatiently.

"You said she was driving, Sayara." I paused as my mind tried to comprehend everything she was saying. "Did she get in an accident and hurt someone? Did someone die?" The thought was frightening.

"No, Maddie, she was DRIVING. Herself. Behind the steering wheel." Sayara was exasperated with me by now.

I was seriously missing something. "Okay, Sayara. She was driving. Was she speeding a lot?" I mean, that's against the law, but you're supposed to get a ticket, not arrested for speeding.

"No!" Sayara threw her hands in the air as she stood up ready to go somewhere, but unclear which direction or how.

"Okay, what gives?" I was genuinely confused.

"Maddie, you don't know anything about my country. Women are not allowed to drive. It's against the law. Themi is in jail. It's just terrible. My poor, beautiful cousin is in a disgusting prison." Her soft voice was shaky, and Sayara was nearly in tears. She sat back down, her shoulders drooped forward.

"What?" I was very confused. "She's in jail because she drove a car?" Where did Sayara come from? Outer space? People drive everywhere. Women drive everywhere. I can't wait to drive. Dad's promised me a car when I get my license. When I was little, I actually wanted to be a race-car driver for a while.

"Maddie, I know it sounds really odd. But there are a lot of awful rules in my country, and one of them is that women can't drive," Sayara gently explained. "Themi has always thought the rule was wrong and unfair. She feels that all women should have the same rights as men. So if men can drive, why can't a woman? Themi wants to drive and so she did, but it's illegal and she broke the law."

"Sounds like a dumb law, if you ask me." I was clearly not understanding these strange laws. "It seems like Themi was protesting an unfair law. How else can you point out that something is wrong if you don't protest against it?"

"It's really dumb, but she can't just protest without consequences. In the kingdom, protests are not allowed, not like in your country. Now my dad is worried about our family's safety, and he wants me home. So I have to go," Sayara sadly informed me.

"It's so weird, Sayara. When my sister Angie turned sixteen, she got her own car." I was still trying to process the craziness of the information she had just given me.

"In my country, Maddie, she would be arrested."

"That's so horrible!" I don't always like Angie, but I would never want to see her hurt or arrested. Why should Angie and Themi have such different lives as girls just because of where they live? I was so glad I lived in a place where I could one day drive and not be arrested. How scary.

"I know it sounds dreadful. I do love my home and my family, but there are some rules that I don't like. Right now I have to go home and help Themi."

"How? How can you help her?" My mind began to spin with ideas of how we could help Themi. I had only known Sayara for a few days, but we had already become very close friends and her problems seemed like my own.

"I don't know, Maddie, but whenever I wanted to do something, Themi always defended me to my mom and dad. I have to do the same for her now. I don't know how. But I have to. She's my cousin, and I love her." Tears were now flowing down her face. Sayara was heartbroken by the thought of her favorite cousin all alone in some dangerous jail.

I had to help, too. I didn't know how, but I knew I just had to. "Sayara, tell me when you're home. I'm going to help you. We can break her out of jail." I had heard people say that in the movies all the time, although I wasn't so sure what that meant.

The corners of Sayara's mouth turned up in a small smile. "Oh, Maddie, you say such ridiculous things! You can't break her out of jail. Her own father is a very important man in the kingdom, and even he is worried for her. What can you do?

What can I do? We're just girls. But this is my family's problem, and I must be there for my family."

"Sayara, you're my friend now, and friends stick together. I don't know what or how, but we'll figure out something to help Themi. And besides, as Aunt AK reminds me all the time, believe in girl power!" I wished Aunt AK was there. She was so much better at handling these kinds of things. She always knew just the right thing to say.

Sayara smiled and said quietly, "There is no value for girl power where I come from. This isn't some silly Supergirl movie. Please, Maddie, tell no one. My father is worried that people will find out, and that will make it more embarrassing for the king and possibly even worse for Themi. This has to stay between us for now. Let me go home, and I'll let you know what's going on. My dad has sent the jet, and we'll be home by tomorrow. I'll video-chat with you as soon as I can."

Chapter 3

Waiting for Sayara to text me felt like a gazillion years. With her gone, the island seemed boring and dull. Luckily we left the next day for home, since spring break was almost over. Linda spent more time with me, which was nice because I know she would have preferred to just sit and read. She clucked over me like a mom, which was a little annoying sometimes, because I felt like she forgot that I was thirteen! So not a little kid. I know, I know, she just loves me, as she tells me all the time.

Even Jason realized that something wasn't right for me with Sayara gone, and he was nicer. Well, not really nicer, just less annoying—but that in itself was nicer. He stayed with his resort buddies and didn't bother me. I was glad Angie wasn't vacationing with us. She would not have been sympathetic and would have immediately told Mom, who would have declared Sayara "an inappropriate friendship" for me since Themi had been arrested. Mom would have made me stop talking to Sayara. Mom could be very opinioned on who I was allowed to talk to. I guess we had some strict and unfair rules in the family, too.

My mind kept going back to Sayara, wondering if she was okay and if her cousin, Themi, was still in jail. Who goes to jail for driving? It was just crazy! I couldn't understand any of it.

A day later, after arriving at home, I walked in the front door and was happily surprised to see Aunt AK. With a giant hug, she said, "Your dad asked me to come hang out for the night.

He had an unexpected business trip and will be back tomorrow. And ..." She paused. "Your mom added another spa treatment, which supposedly will last another day." Her eyes rolled slightly as she and Linda exchanged knowing glances. They always think I don't see those silent mental connections, but I see all!

Aunt AK thinks my mom neglects me and Jason. I heard her complain to my dad once when she thought no one was listening. But sometimes being neglected is better than being harassed, and these days it seems my mom nags me about everything, so I'm kinda happy when she isn't around.

I love my mom, but I don't always like her. We just have such different viewpoints and opinions, and she can't understand me at all. Nor does she even try. She just dictates orders, most of which don't even apply or make sense. And when we disagree, she just yells and then silent-treatments me. And she calls *me* the child! Aunt AK seems so much more reasonable, even when she's upset with me—we talk it out, and there's no silent treatment ever.

"So Mads and Jason, it's just us and party time." There was a familiar twinkle in Aunt AK's eye. "We're gonna let Linda have some time off to go see her family, too."

"Excellent," I exclaimed. Hanging with Aunt AK was the best and just what I needed.

"So, kids, how was the resort? Jason, how cool were the waterslides? And, Maddie, tell me more about your new vacation friend Sayara."

I had forgotten that I had texted Aunt AK pictures of us on the waterslides. The happy pictures had been taken before Sayara's world turned upside down on her.

"The water rides were awesome, they were—" Jason began but stopped midsentence as he was distracted by the texts on his phone.

17

"And? They were? What, Jason?" Aunt AK quizzed.

"What?" Jason asked with a blank stare. Clearly his friends' chats were more interesting.

"Never mind, you can tell me later. Go hang with your friends. Dinner's in two hours, but have a snack now if you're hungry." She rattled off the instructions knowing that his attention was long gone and only growls from a hungry tummy would eventually bring him back.

"So, just you and me, Maddie-girl," said Aunt AK, using the pet name Linda had given me long ago. Everyone in my family liked using it. Aunt AK said it fit me since I was a little bohemian and a free spirit, just like her. Aunt AK hugged my shoulders as we walked into the family room.

"Lots to tell," I said, realizing I needed to talk to Aunt AK privately. Luckily Jason was already well on his way to the media room, wanting to game with his friends online.

"How was the trip and your friend Sayara? You've been very vague the last two days. Did you have a fight with her? It's not like you to argue," Aunt AK probed.

"No, not at all!" I sighed. "Oh, Aunt AK, it's a mess, but not my mess, and I am so worried for Sayara. Prison is a terrible place, and I don't know how to help!" The words tumbled from my mouth at lightning speed, jumbled and confused just as the thoughts bounced around in my mind.

"Prison? Whoa, Maddie. Sayara's in prison?" Aunt AK's eyebrows went up, and she gave me that look she gives me when she's more worried about me than whatever else is going on. "Why don't you tell me everything and slowly. Start from the beginning." Aunt AK's calm voice was reassuring as we settled onto the large, cushy sofa by the bay window.

So I started at day one about how Sayara and I met over my hair. Aunt AK smiled. "I have told you, Maddie, that your hair is just one part of who are you. And the color, that's just a sign of how special and unique you are inside." Aunt AK always knows just what to say to make me feel better, even though I still haven't decided to believe her or not. Still, it was what I needed to hear.

I continued to tell her about how Sayara and I spent every day together and then the surprising news about Themi. Aunt AK nodded.

"Ah, I see, so Themi broke the official rule in the kingdom. It's not fair, Maddie, I know. Governments in every country make laws that are not always sensible or fair to everyone. The driving ban against women in the kingdom is one of those. Women there have been trying to fight against it for a while. Some of them try to drive and then get arrested, like Themi. She's very brave, and I can see why you want to support her. But it's not so easy. These situations are very complicated," explained Aunt AK.

"I don't see why it's so complicated," I complained. As far as I was concerned, this was as easy as it comes. Dumb law, get rid of it. "Why don't they just get rid of the law? It's not fair, and it's not right. Women around the world drive, and they should be able to in the kingdom. Do those same women get to drive when they come here?" I wondered about what would happen to Themi if she were here.

"Maddie, you have a sharp mind, and you're right. Themi could drive anytime she wanted to here or in any other country where there's no discrimination against women driving. But she doesn't live here—she lives with her family in the kingdom, and it's complicated when there are rules that are old or unreasonable. It takes very brave, wise people to recognize when old traditions are sometimes not only unjust but morally wrong. Telling young girls like Themi that they can't do something as basic as driving is a very unfair practice." Aunt AK sighed as she explained.

Suddenly my eyes widened as a brilliant idea flashed through my mind. "Then that's what we have to do, Aunt AK. We'll bring Themi here, and she can live with us and drive whenever she wants," I declared with the smug satisfaction of having solved the problem so quickly.

"It would be nice if the world were so simple," smiled Aunt AK, "but there are many complicating factors. First, Themi is in jail from what you say. Second, her whole life and family are in the kingdom, and she may not want to live far away from them. She probably wants to be treated equally at home. This is about a lot more than just driving. Driving is really a symbol for Themi and her friends. They probably just want the same freedoms as young women everywhere."

Bzzzz. A text on my phone. "It's Sayara! Finally!" I was surprised and excited. "She says she can video-chat in ten minutes. Wanna meet her?" I asked.

"I'd love to," Aunt AK said. "I'm getting some lemonade—would you like some snacks? I'll take some to Jason, too. Dinner is in two hours, and you can help me cook."

"A snack sounds great. I'm starving," I declared. I was happy Aunt AK would be cooking. She's a great cook like my dad, and I love helping her.

"You're always hungry, Maddie. Where do you put all that food? It's good that you play so many sports," noted Aunt AK. It's true—I love to eat and I love to play almost every sport, although soccer and basketball are my favorites.

Just as we were walking into the kitchen to get snacks, the doorbell rang. It was Mikey.

"Hey, Mikey." I high-fived him as he walked in. His big noise-canceling headphones were perched on his head, and he was jamming to a beat I couldn't hear.

"Whatsup?" He nodded to me and then turned very politely to Aunt AK and said, "Hi, Aunt AK." Mikey has known Aunt

AK since we were very little. He lives four houses down the street, and we've been buddies since our first day of preschool. He's one of my two best friends. I know it's weird, since he's a boy. But I don't really think about that, and neither does he. Aunt AK calls us her three musketeers, "muskies" for short— Mikey, Mila, and me. Inseparable. Usually.

"So, you're finally back, Maddie," he said to me, but not really listening and still looking at his phone. "Look at this dope video that Timmy sent me."

"Uh, yeah, later. Hey, listen, I met this girl and I have to video-chat with her now," I said, not sure if he wanted to hang around while I talked to Sayara. He pulled off his headphones, angling his phone toward me.

"Okay, whatever," Mikey said as he walked into the family room and plopped down on the sofa. Mikey settled in like the family he was. Clearly there would be no privacy. Whatever. It didn't matter, as Mikey and I didn't really have secrets anyhow.

My tablet chimed and I clicked the green phone button. A gentle voice called my name. "Maddie, hi." It took a second before Sayara's face moved in front of her camera.

"You look so tired and sad." Words tumbled from my mouth before I could think clearly. Always my problem.

"Uh, thanks a lot, Maddie!" Sayara answered crossly. "You'd look like this too if you'd come home to all I've had to deal with." Her eyes were tearing in frustration.

"I'm sorry, Sayara. I didn't mean to be rude—I'm just used to seeing you so happy. We were having so much fun," I apologized. What else could I do? The words were already out of my big mouth. "How's all?" I tried to nonchalantly ask.

"It's still such a mess. Themi spent a whole day in the women's prison. Luckily, her dad is powerful, so he pulled some strings and got her home. She's now at her home under house confinement. That really just means 'arrest,' but my dad says it sounds better. Themi's father is furious with her. Keeps saying she has blackened the family name. My dad doesn't want me around her—he says she's a bad influence on me, which is totally ridiculous." Her voice choked with frustration.

"I'm so glad she's home, Sayara." I was relieved to hear that Themi was no longer in jail. "I've been so worried … and since I didn't hear from you, I didn't know if you were in jail, too," I said.

"That would be silly—I didn't do anything against the law, Maddie. I would never go to jail. But Themi is always trying to change things, and my dad said it's her own fault for trying to push for reform before people are ready," said Sayara matter-of-factly, parroting what she had heard from the grown-ups around her. I was surprised at this side of Sayara. She had been so independent and free-spirited on vacation. When we had been together, Sayara had constantly complained about how trapped she felt in her life. She wanted to drive race cars and fly to the moon, literally! And now she was acting all critical of Themi. What gives? I wondered.

"It's not completely her fault," intervened Aunt AK from behind me.

"Sayara, this is Aunt AK, who I told you about," I said as I introduced them.

"Oh, hello, Miss Aunt AK," said Sayara formally, sitting up a bit straighter.

"Geez, Sayara, you don't have to be so formal. It's just Aunt AK," I giggled.

"Oh, Sayara, it's nice to meet you, and don't worry, I understand. Maddie, Sayara is just trying to be respectful as she knows I'm lots older than you both. Thank you, Sayara," Aunt AK explained.

Okay, now I felt like the goofy kid. Foot in mouth again!

"Hey, what about me?" Mikey piped up from behind, not leaving the sofa but sticking his head up past my left shoulder.

"Sayara, this is my buddy Mikey," I said as I pointed to him.

"Mikey? There's a boy in your living room?" Sayara questioned with surprise in her voice.

"Uh, yeah." What was up with Sayara? She seemed so formal and different from when we were hanging out on vacation.

"Sorry, I'm just not used to that. Here we can't have any boys in the same room, unless they're a relative," Sayara explained.

"There's sure a lot of weird, strict rules where you live, Sayara," I said, shaking my head.

"Actually, Maddie, they only seem harsh to you because they're different," explained Aunt AK. "In the kingdom, there's more respect for older people, which is why Sayara called me 'Miss' when just 'Aunt AK' is fine. Some people think that rules against girls and boys in the same room are there to make sure everyone stays safe and makes good choices. It's a little like when I was in university—no boys were allowed anywhere in my dorm house beyond the main floor. But people realized that the rules were unnecessarily strict and changed them. Besides, people realized that it's also good for boys and girls to learn how to be friends and respect each other equally early on in life. Makes it easier when you grow up and have to work with one another and have the same opportunities."

"You mean that Mikey and I couldn't hang out in the kingdom?" I asked. I had traveled a lot with my family and had seen that people in most countries around the world have their own way of doing things, but I was still hung up on all the strict and crazy rules in the kingdom. They seemed much harsher than the rules of other places I had visited.

"Probably not," admitted Aunt AK.

"That would totally stink," said Mikey as he finally got up and walked over to me and Aunt AK. Looking into the tablet for the first time, he saw Sayara and suddenly he stood up a little straighter. "Uh, hi, are you Sayara?" he asked with a deeper voice, clearly pleased with what he saw. His hand brushed the side of his hair as he made a sudden attempt to be charming and smooth. I rolled my eyes, and Aunt AK chuckled.

"Hi, Mikey," Sayara replied. "Yes, I'm Sayara. I didn't realize you were the same Mikey Maddie talked about. I had pictured some weird, goofy, little neighborhood kid."

"Thanks a lot, Maddie," Mikey said, a little annoyed as he fake-punched my arm with a scowl on his face. "Actually, I go by Michael now," he informed us all matter-of-factly in his fake grown-up voice.

"Uh, since when?" I was unimpressed at his lame attempt to be serious. What was he talking about?

"Uh, since this break. I realized that we're going to be in high school in the fall, and I need to start sounding grown-up." He lowered and deepened his voice even further for effect.

I stuck my finger in my mouth and pretended to gag because it was so ridiculous. Mikey was my buddy, and Sayara was my new friend. Eww. Even Aunt AK snickered.

"Uh, whatever. Hey, Sayara," I switched the subject to what I really cared about, "so what's going to happen to Themi?" This was intense. A friend's cousin under house arrest—and for driving a car! I was still having trouble getting my head around it all.

"Well, she's at home, but she'll have to go before the judgment council so they can decide if she should be punished. There were eight different women who chose to protest the dumb law, and all of them have been arrested. The other seven are still in jail. My uncle says that the king can't release just Themi without punishment, even though their family has connections, because it will set a bad example for the others who may try to keep protesting," explained Sayara.

"What happens in house arrest?" Mikey asked.

"She can't leave the house, but at least she's safe and has her own room, her bed, and food. But the judgment council is concerned that she'll still be able to get online and spread her ideas about the driving ban. They have forbidden her from being online in any way. So her dad took away her phone and computer. My father said the jail is terrible, dirty, and has no proper beds, showers, or food—so Themi should be grateful that her family intervened and she is now at home under their protection. But Themi is very worried about her friends." Sayara's voice crackled with emotion, and tears filled her soft brown eyes. I was beginning to see just how much Sayara cared about her favorite cousin. "They might be given lashes, and Themi might as well, if she doesn't obey …"

"Lashes? You mean like with a cane or stick?" I was stunned. I had read about these things in a book about the ancient medieval times, but I couldn't imagine they were being done to kids living in the world today!

"Okay, kids," Aunt AK intervened. Thank goodness. I couldn't handle any more of this talk. "This is a lot for all of us to digest. Sayara, are you okay, honey? It's probably really late where you are, around 10:30 p.m., since you're seven hours ahead of us. Time for bed for you," she said with a gentle, soothing voice. "Maddie, you can talk to Sayara tomorrow." And with that Aunt AK urged us with her eyes to say goodbye.

"Yes, it's late," Sayara said softly. "Later, Maddie."

"Don't worry, Sayara, we'll figure out a way to help you," I offered. How exactly, I didn't know. But I needed to let her know that I wanted to help.

After another minute of sad goodbyes, we all clicked off.

"Maddie, how are you gonna help her?" Mikey asked.

"Uh, yeah. I don't know how, but somehow, we gotta help her and Themi. We can't just do nothing."

"You're crazy as always. You're always trying to fix everything for everyone, but this is way out of your league." He was used to my schemes, but his annoyed eyes and raised eyebrows expressed his disbelief. "We're in a different country, and we can't just go over there and bring her here."

"Maddie, honey, I have to agree with Mikey on this one. I know you want to help a friend in need, save the world and all, but some things are beyond our control."

"How can you say that, Aunt AK? You always tell me that we have to help people in need and go the distance. Well, we gotta go the distance. It's not fair that Themi's life should be so different just because of where she was born. Wouldn't you want someone to do this for me if I was stuck in some jail or under house arrest for protesting dumb laws?" My exasperated voice rose in volume.

"Maddie, I know it seems so simple to you, but these issues are very complicated," Aunt AK said, trying to reason with me. But she could tell that I was in what my dad calls my "stubborn mode."

"It is simple, and people need to talk it through like at the peace table at school," I began to explain. The peace table was something our school did even in first grade. If kids disagreed, they had to go to the peace table and talk until they solved their problem. And if they couldn't, then other kids could get involved and help them. My teacher said the goal was to learn to talk through our problems, not just argue and fight.

"Talking will solve it," I said, confident of my opinion. "Everyone will come to realize that it is not a fair rule. Someone just needs to talk to the king and that judgment council and make them see things from the girls' point of view, and

26

then they will realize that this driving ban is an unfair law." As I uttered the words, a plan began to take shape in my mind. I smiled to myself. *I* would go to talk to the king and the judgment council. How? I wasn't sure … yet. But those were just tiny details, and I wasn't usually one for details. I was more focused on the big scheme, and my secret plan was already starting to form.

Chapter 4

The next morning, the school bus came on time at 7:30 a.m., but I had already been awake for two hours. My mind was whirring with how to secretly get to the kingdom so that I could persuade the king to fix the stupid driving law. It was all I could think of.

Bouncing onto the bus, I saw Mila on the left side in the middle. As always, there was an open seat next to her just for me. It had been that way since kindergarten.

"Hey, Mila!" I said. I was thrilled to see my best friend. Mikey may be one of us three muskies, but Mila is my soul sister. Actually, her name is Camila, but I started calling her Mila in preschool, and now her whole family calls her Mila.

"Hey, Maddie!" Mila moved her backpack so I could sit down. "How was break?"

"Awesome! Did you dance the whole break?" I asked. I've always been in awe of her dedication. I'm pretty devoted to soccer and basketball, but nothing like Mila. She eats and breathes ballet. Mila has wanted to be a ballerina since I can remember. We both started dance lessons in preschool, but I switched to soccer as soon as I could.

"Yep, all break. But it was fun. Tell me all about the Bahamas and that huge water park. Any cute boys?" She giggled. Mila was already wondering about boys and stuff. But I really didn't notice them. Most of the boys my age were still annoying and usually disgusting.

"No cute boys, or at least I didn't notice," I said matter-of-factly, to which Mila rolled her eyes at me.

"Oh, Maddie, you never notice these things!"

"Yeah, but I met this really cool girl whose cousin is …" I leaned over to whisper in her ear.

"In jail!" Mila exclaimed.

"Shhh, don't let everyone hear that!" I said quickly, glancing around. Luckily everyone was still "break hungover"—our term for being sleepy and tired and wishing that it was still spring break.

"What gives?" Mila whispered. "Details, girl!" And with that, I told Mila the fast version in the ten-minute bus ride to school.

"That's the wildest story I have ever heard, Maddie!" Mila exclaimed as I finished with the last details. "So sad, too. Poor Sayara."

"I know," I told Mila. "But I'm going to help them. I'm gonna find a way to get there, Mila."

"Maddie, you're crazy—you can't go there! What if they put you in jail?" Mila said both in a fearful whisper and in the sternest tone possible.

"Me, in jail? For what?" It hadn't occurred to me that there might be a downside to my plan.

"Maddie, you're nuts, as always. If you sneak into the kingdom, maybe they'll arrest you for breaking some weird rules. Promise me you won't do anything stupid. You can't go, that's all there is," Mila said bossily. Usually I don't mind her bossiness, but I did right then.

"Mila, if you were in trouble, wouldn't you expect me to do whatever I could to help you?"

"Maddie, I would never be in jail, so that's a stupid question because it doesn't apply. I would never ask you to do something illegal!" Mila could be stubborn.

Me in jail? I hadn't thought that through. Okay, so there was just one more potential problem I would have to plan around. I had to make sure that my scheme was truly a secret and I couldn't break any rules … well, at least I had to make sure I didn't land in jail!

Chapter 5

That night, I was doing homework in the kitchen. I've always liked it better in there. In Mila's house, everyone hangs out in the kitchen, no matter what they're doing. Mila's family is so much closer than mine. Everyone teases one another, and every Saturday night they play cards and board games. I love sleeping over on game night, and I have pretty good luck with the card games! Mila's mom always makes the best food and desserts. She's always trying to get us to eat more, even when our stomachs are ready to burst. But I love when she makes her homemade apple pie sundaes—apple pie topped with fresh brownies, vanilla ice cream, and hot fudge. It's the best treat ever.

Here in my house, it's usually just me studying and Linda cooking and chatting. Linda has become my mom in a way, even though she didn't give birth to me. When I was little, Linda did everything for me: fed me, took me to school, did homework with me, made the best cut-out costumes from cardboard boxes, read to me, everything.

Mom would pop her head in once in a while and sometimes joined us at my toddler classes, but she never really played with me at the park or read to me at night. Linda always made my favorite foods. When I was sick, she sat with me and watched all the corny television shows I loved. Linda planned all my birthday parties, and she was always there to help me finish every homework project. She has her own daughters, but she always has plenty of love for all of us. I used to call Linda "Mom" when I was little until she made me stop. I realized it was because she was worried about hurting Mom's feelings.

Once Mom and I even got into a fight about it, and she threatened to fire Linda. I learned quickly to never raise the issue. Protecting Linda was more important to me than calling her "Mom." Mom sometimes yelled at her, which I hated. Just because someone works for you doesn't mean you can be rude to them. But to Mom, Linda will always be the "help." Only Dad understands, but he's always too nice to confront Mom. He just tries to lighten everyone's mood with nonstop jokes.

It was odd how similar Sayara and I felt about our families. Our moms are perfectly fine people, but both got stuck being moms because that's the only thing that was expected of them. They've always assumed that we will grow up and live lives just like theirs. But I don't want that, and neither does Sayara. Her mom wants her to study hard in school, but university would only come after she's married. Sayara said it's all about protecting the family's reputation and honor, so in the kingdom, everyone wants the girls married off early. Sayara said one of her cousins was seventeen and they made her marry a really old guy who was like thirty! So not for me. I wonder what they will make Sayara do.

I felt bad that I hadn't told Linda about Themi being in jail, but I had to keep this quiet. Only Aunt AK was safe. Linda was trustworthy, but I knew that it was sometimes hard with Mom as her boss, so I didn't want to make Linda's life tougher if Mom asked her questions. She could honestly say she didn't know anything.

I was crunching through a second set of geometry problems when I heard Dad come through the garage door.

"Where's my favorite little sunburst?" a voice called from the doorway.

"Daddy!" I leapt into his arms—and thank goodness he was more than tall and strong enough to catch all five feet four inches of me.

"Whoa, Maddie, you're gonna tackle me," laughed Dad. He turned to Linda. "Hi, Linda, how are you? Thanks for holding down the fort while I was away."

"You're welcome, Roger," Linda said with a smile. "Dinner's almost ready. Why don't you both have fun catching up while I put some laundry in the dryer?" And with that Linda gave my dad and me some alone time. Linda always said it was very special to have time together, just the two of us. She knew it was hard on me when Mom was around.

"Hey, squirt, how was the Bahamas?" Dad asked, yanking gently on my ponytail. He always called me any one of a bunch of pet names. It was our playful way, making pet names for each other.

"Oh, Dad, it was fun, but I missed you!" I hugged him again. It was always more fun when Dad was on vacation with us. He'd take us out in the boat and we'd snorkel around. Linda gets seasick, so she hates to be on boats. "Jason was only marginally annoying," I informed him, "and I met a new friend, Sayara. Her family is just like ours—she has an older sister and a younger brother, too—and she loves fast waterslides."

"That's great." Dad beamed with the satisfaction of hearing that we had a good time. "I'm sorry I couldn't join you on this spring break, but I'll make it up to you this summer, I promise, kiddo."

"That's okay, Dad, I understand that you gotta work," I replied, all-knowing in my pretend grown-up voice.

"Thanks, little Maddie, you seem to be more understanding than your mom these days. You're getting big and mature way too fast for me." His voice was a little sad as he played with the end of my ponytail.

"Dad," I reminded him as I rolled my eyes. "Hello. I'm thirteen. I'm going to be in high school next year—you have to start treating me like an adult, or at least a real teen."

"Oh, yes," he teased, "a big high-school girl who still rolls her eyes." His voice was playful as he tugged at my ponytail. "But you'll always be daddy's little girl." Why did everyone want me to stay their little girl?

"Oh, Dad, seriously. Just accept it. I'm almost a woman," I stated.

Before he could stop laughing, in came my mom. "What's so funny?" She tried to sound interested, but it was clear she was only asking to be polite.

"Maddie was just telling me that she's almost a woman," Dad informed her.

"That's sweet, honey," Mom said with her mouth, but her beautiful, perfectly made-up, distracted eyes glanced at me disapprovingly. Something in my looks had not met her satisfaction, but she wasn't going to trouble herself to say much. That would change the focus from her to me, and she wasn't interested in that.

My mom once told me that she had had us kids because that was pretty much what was expected of her by the age of twenty-five. In her family, it was expected that all well-raised girls got married to nice, rich men who would take care of them while they stayed home and had babies. My mother could have chosen differently. She had plenty of options to choose a career and be a mom. But my mother was a reluctant mom, only because she had to be one. And careers, well, that's not really her thing, either. Truthfully, Mom just seems to want to be taken care of, like that's her real life goal. I don't know if that's okay, but it's definitely not for me. I want something different.

One day, I'd love to have a big family that hangs out and has fun, like Mikey's or Mila's. Both of them have a mom who is everything I wish my mom could be. I know I should be saying how great Mom is—isn't that what most people expect? But I can't. I love her because she's my mom, but I don't always understand her. And she doesn't always treat Linda or some of the people who work for Dad nicely, which I don't like. Everyone's equal, aren't they? Mom's not a bad person or anything like that and she can be nice to some people, especially when she wants something from them. I just wish she'd love me as is. We assume that our parents are great, nice, right about everything, and perfect—until one day we realize that maybe they're not.

And if it weren't for Aunt AK and Linda, I would be a mess—even more than I sometimes feel! Aunt AK stepped in and mothered each of us as if we were her own. Isn't that an irony of life? My mom could have kids and she didn't really want them. And because of her cancer, Aunt AK couldn't have any of her own kids, so she treated us like her own children.

"Well, everyone, I have just had the most amazing week," Mom announced to Dad and me.

"That's wonderful, honey. Did you enjoy the spa, too?" Dad asked absentmindedly. His attention had already shifted to some other topic in his mind before the words were fully out of his mouth. The smile on his face remained warm, but you could tell by the glaze in his eyes that he had lost interest.

Dad indulged Mom but mainly because he was busy with his ambitions. He had been raised completely differently, where education and hard work mattered most and everyone in the family supported each other in pursuit of those twin goals.

Only Aunt AK had managed to find the balance and have some fun along with it. She said it was because she had faced some hard knocks with her cancer and not being able to have her own kids. She said when you are denied something you want very much, you come to appreciate the randomness of life and fate and more. I think I'm still trying to understand what all that really means.

My mother's shallow words filled the kitchen. "The treatments were great, and my skin—can't you tell?—they said it looks ten years younger." Mom caressed her own cheek. "And the yoga meditation, divine. I actually think I achieved enlightenment. I have found my third eye," she smugly declared, referring to the all-knowing insight that supposedly comes with meditation and yoga.

From anyone more serious, it might have been believable, but from my mom … it was as ridiculous a statement as any she made. But Mom genuinely lived life on the surface, and for her, "enlightenment" really just meant that she had paid a ton of money to be very well taken care of by the dutiful folks at the spa center, and so she was feeling good, very good. Aunt AK said that Mom thought that spiritual mindfulness was something to be bought as easily as a pair of yoga pants. By this point, Dad and I were well accustomed to these bizarre announcements from Mom after every retreat, and we just laughed silently when she wasn't looking.

Mom was forever following the trend of the moment, pretending to be all spiritual with her meditation or whatever, but it was always on the surface. Never deep down inside, and if I asked any questions she didn't like, I usually got the silent treatment as if I had somehow been disrespectful for questioning her thinking, something I wished she did more naturally.

"That's nice, honey," Dad said flippantly. "How about we enlighten our stomachs with some food? I'm starving." I was still laughing into my math book.

"Where's Linda? It's her responsibility to make sure dinner's ready on time," Mom said dismissively. "I don't cook—you know that, honey," she reminded him matter-of-factly, as if to reconfirm that her place in our home was definitely not in the kitchen.

Mom is still fighting the old stereotypes of women with one hand and with the other hand, reinforcing them with Angie and me. On one hand, she wants us to study hard and be good at sports, but on the flip side, she's worried that I, in particular, will never find a nice, rich boy to marry, which in her mind is the only real goal for a girl. I'm too wild and independent in my thoughts, she says. Boys will be intimidated by me, and I need to dim my energy a little so I don't scare them off. Only my secret guardian angel Aunt AK tells me that this is hogwash and malarkey—and I should be focused on being the best person I can be and not worry about silly, outdated things. "Never compromise yourself or your ideals, Maddie," she always says. "Parents love us, but sometimes their ideas and opinions are outdated. Outdated thinking with an expiration date on it," she'd exclaim. "Pour that spoiled thinking down the drain and focus on learning how to think for yourself, not just blindly believing everything grown-ups tell you."

Besides, Aunt AK says that with more than seven billion people in the world, there will definitely be a guy that will be a good fit for me when the time is right. Years and years and years from now! I'm in no rush.

It was just like in health class when Miss Baker would tell us that we shouldn't worry about what other people think of us or how we look or act. "As long as you act according to your values and are respectful of other people, you will be fine in life." Her raspy voice would ring louder than expected from her tiny little body, her wire glasses perched off the edge of her bumpy nose. "Treat people like you want to be treated, and you're less likely to have problems with people." It was her gospel, and she repeated it every time someone complained about someone else.

I already knew I was outgrowing my mom and her old-fashioned ideas. My dad gave me hope and support, but sometimes he bent to the will of my mom.

"Hello … Maddie … where are you?" Dad's knuckles fake-knocked on my forehead. "You get lost in your thoughts, Mads. What are you thinking?"

"Sorry, Dad. Nothing, just school," I replied. Lame, I know, but I couldn't tell him how I felt about Mom. It would crush him to think that she wasn't as doting as she led him to believe. He relied on her for the "parenting" thing, and for his sake, I'd keep pretending all was okay.

Perhaps I would test the water with him about Sayara. "I was also thinking about what Sayara told me about the kingdom. Did you know that girls are not allowed to drive there?"

"Yes, it's a terrible situation. Very complicated, and it'll take time to change those old laws. People need to be patient."

"How long? It must stink for the women today who can't drive. How long do they have to wait?" I questioned.

"Oh, Maddie," my mother piped in. "You're so impatient. And besides, the kingdom's very far away and not our problem. Don't worry yourself about other people's problems."

"Mom!" She could always exasperate me so quickly. "Somebody has to care!" I declared, knowing full well my mother really never cared about anything that didn't directly impact her.

"Oh, Maddie, you can't fix everything. Well, maybe your father can write a check to some charity that can help." My mother's answer to everything was money—more accurately, my dad's money. Waving her fingers dismissively, she turned her attention back to making her vegetable smoothie.

My dad's eyebrows raised, but I felt the need to speak before he did.

"Mom, Sayara doesn't need money! She has tons. She needs our help."

"Maddie," my dad's soothing voice intervened, "I think what your mother meant is that she would rather just give a donation to some group that is helping the girls. This works sometimes, but not all the time. Like in this case. The kingdom is very wealthy, as you said about Sayara, but they need to value girls as much as boys. Those kinds of changes in values and people's attitudes take a lot longer. That's what I meant about patience. But I agree with you, Maddie, it must stink for Sayara and her friends who are living with the restrictions right now." Dad paused and then looked back at me. "Is that what you and Sayara talked about? How did it come up, since neither of you are old enough to drive anywhere in the world?"

Okay, dangerous direction for this conversation. I could not tell them about Themi being arrested. Mom would ban me from talking to Sayara, since she'd incorrectly conclude that anyone with a family member who had been arrested must be from a *bad* family. Mom often has a false sense of righteousness.

"It was just something that came up because I mentioned when Angie got her driver's license and how I can't wait to get mine!"

"Oh, I see," my dad muttered. A new text on his phone had already distracted him.

Smooth, I congratulated myself as I threw them off the trail of the real reason for my quiet focus. How was I going to help Sayara? Doing nothing would be terrible and something I have never been capable of, anyhow. I really didn't understand all of the issues, but I knew I had to go to Sayara and figure out how to help Themi avoid any punishment. I needed to find a way to talk to the king and the judgment council and make them see how ridiculous these laws against girls were.

While pondering the options, my ears perked up when my mom informed my dad, "Don't forget, honey, I'm taking my sisters to that new spa next week. We leave on Saturday morning." Mom's two favorite pastimes, traveling and being pampered.

Perfect. She would be gone. One parent out of the picture.

"Oh, Anita, I forgot that was next week. I have a conference in San Francisco … it looks like Linda will be on duty."

This was too good to be true. Mom and Dad gone, with only Linda to manage. Much easier. What excuse could I give? Then it came to me—I'd just say that I had a sleepover on Saturday! I would go to Mila's, and she could cover for me. No one would even miss me for a few days if I worked it out right. I had four days to plan it all. Now all I needed to do was book a flight. My mind raced with the extra details. Luckily I knew the passwords my mom usually used with her mileage account. This might actually work!

Chapter 6

The rest of the week passed by in a bit of a planning blur. I knew I had to get to the kingdom, and using Mom's miles to book my ticket online was even easier than I realized.

I knew that Mila would be worried, and she was. But she already felt terrible for Themi, and she was always a sap for anyone in need—and besides, there was our muskie oath to protect and defend each other. We usually used it against the annoying mean kids at school, but I knew she'd totally be on my side about taking action when she heard my story about Themi and jail.

On Wednesday, I went to Mila's house after soccer tryouts. Technically I was already on the team as I was every year, but the coach made us all try out to be fair to any new kids. Mila danced every afternoon now so she couldn't play soccer anymore. But I loved soccer, and basketball was a close second. It was hard to choose sometimes, but I really wanted to play varsity in high school so I practiced wicked hard.

I had messaged Sayara about soccer tryouts, and she told me she wished she could play on a team. I was so surprised to hear that her school had no teams for girls. Girls our age couldn't play anymore in the kingdom. Another unfair thing. No sports in public for girls, but boys were allowed to play anything they wanted. It didn't seem right. Sayara had secretly learned to play from their driver, Rajiv, but her mother found out and yelled at her and the driver for putting Sayara in such a position of wearing shorts and exposing herself. I don't see what the big deal is, but Sayara lives in the land of crazy rules and so our lives are completely different just because of where we were born.

I walked into Mila's side door from the garage. It went straight into the mudroom, where I dumped my muddy soccer shoes and my backpack. I walked into the kitchen, which was cozy and smelled like fresh cookies. Oh, yum! I love going to Mila's house. Actually, I love hanging out at both Mila's and Mikey's houses. Mikey's mom and dad are both lawyers. They met in law school, but they're not boring or anything like that. They're actually kinda fun to talk to and hang out with. They're also into camping and hiking. Sometimes they take Mila and me with them.

A warm voice welcomed me, interrupting my thoughts. "Hi, Maddie!" Mila's mom greeted me from behind with a big bear hug. "You're just in time, honey—I just baked cookies, new recipe, and you have to try some. Mila will be home shortly." That's the nice thing about Mila's house—everyone welcomes me, even if Mila isn't there. They make me feel like I'm part of the family.

"Hi, Mrs. V, thanks! You don't need to convince me," I said as I piled a few cookies on my plate and grabbed some milk from the fridge.

Mila's so lucky that her mom is like the best mom ever. It was her goal in life to be a mom, have a family, raise kids, and take really good care of everyone. Mila once told me that her mom lost her mom in a car accident when she was ten. She was really sad for many years, but the loss made her want her own big, happy family. Mila's two brothers are already in university, and now she's studying ballet full-time. She's really lucky that her parents totally support her choice.

I can't imagine my mom taking care of me the way Mila's mom does. I think it's because Mila's mom wanted kids and my mom really didn't. Growing up with Aunt AK and

41

Grammy, who's in a wheelchair, I realize that we don't really get to choose what happens to us in life, but I think we get to choose what kind of friend or parent or person we want to be. I sometimes wish I was part of Mila's family, but then I would miss Aunt AK too much. And my dad, I would miss my dad a ton.

Mila's mom is actually a teacher, but she stays home to take care of the kids, especially to help Mila with her dancing. Mila wants to be a prima ballerina for a big dance company one day. That would be really cool. Mila's mom and dad go to every one of her performances. Mila's dad can be a little dorky like mine, but he's still fun, too, plus he makes the best cupcakes in the world. He works on building airplanes and sometimes takes us to visit the factory, which is really neat because I want to learn to fly one day.

Mila's dad used to be our soccer and softball coach when we were little, and my dad would help him out. Dad always came to all my soccer games, but Mom never did. She said that sports were my dad's responsibility, as if taking care of your kids was a chore, not something you loved to do. She only went to Angie's swim meets, but I think that's because she thinks swimming is a better sport for girls than soccer. Mom thinks games like soccer are too rough for girls.

Last year when I made the coed team, I was so mad when all Mom could say was "Time for you to switch to all-girls teams now. You're getting older. You should be on a girls-only team." That was so unfair, especially since I was one of the few girls to make the coed team. If I can make the team fair and square, I should get to be on it. Mom was unreasonable, but Dad stepped in and said that if I was good enough for the coach, I was good enough to be on the team. Period. I was so mad at Mom that day that I went to Mila's to sleep over, just to get out of the house.

As always, Mila's mom had made me see things differently. "Your mom is just being a mom the way she was raised. Just saying the same things to you that were said to her."

Mila's mom reminded me gently, "Your mom loves you, but she probably does so in a way that's different from what you want or need. Some people go on autopilot when they're young and they have kids because that's what they think they're supposed to do. It takes a lot to raise a child—trust me, I know." She paused and then added, "And I totally love it, but it's a lot of work. And not just to make sure that you're all well fed and clothed," she said, tweaking my nose affectionately, "but also to make sure that you grow up to be kind and good inside. We forget about the insides, which are sometimes more important than the outsides."

Just like Aunt AK always said, "It's all about the insides."

I've told Mila's mom on more than one occasion that I wished she was my mom. But she's always been very respectful of my mom. "Oh, sweetie, that's kind of you. You're very lucky to have your own mom and several moms-in-spirit. In a way, I am a little of a mother to you because you're Mila's friend. Your Aunt AK is a really wonderful aunt, and she loves you very much. Just remember in life, you may be lucky to be mothered by people other than the mom who gave birth to you. And that's just as great. It could be your aunt, your grandmother, a teacher, or a friend's mom," she added with a tender wink. Or Linda, I thought.

"But my mom doesn't talk to me like you or Aunt AK do or even Grammy, who's an old-timer but really wise, too," I protested. My mom thinks all our conversations should go in one direction: statements and orders from her to me, never a back-and-forth discussion.

"I know, honey, we assume that all mothers will be the same because that's what we see on TV. Those TV moms who are always there for their kids, caring about their kids, being all cool and fun. And by the end of the show, they always seem to care about what their kids think and all that good stuff. But really, moms are just people and not everyone is the same. And for that matter, not everyone is kind or capable of taking care of other people. We can't assume all moms are the same. Or even that dads are all the same. You can love your mom, but you can accept her faults, too. All of us have shortcomings. And be happy that you're very lucky to have Aunt AK and Grammy in the family who also love to mother you."

At that moment, I was reminded of something that Grammy always said: "Feeding the belly is the easy part; feeding the soul, now that's the real job of a good mom and dad." Aunt AK said that Grammy's only mistake was that she thought everyone would feed the soul with that same kindness and good nature like she did. But in my few short years, I had come to the same conclusion as Aunt AK, that some people were just mean and selfish. Who taught them that? I wondered. Their parents or themselves?

I was thinking about all that when Mila walked in. "I'm starved!" she announced, hugging her mom and then grabbing a plate of cookies. Her mom poured her a glass of milk.

"Hi, honey, was dance good?" her mom asked.

"Yep."

"Homework?"

"Yep."

"Love these one-word answers," her mom said with affectionate sarcasm. "One day, maybe I'll get a full sentence from you!" She winked at me over Mila's head. "All right, girls, there's more warm cookies and some fruit on the counter behind you. Help yourselves. And start your homework in an hour so you're not up too late again. I have some paperwork to go through." Mila's mom was starting to substitute-teach again. She was substituting for my history teacher, Ms. Williams, who just had a baby girl and would be out for five more months until the fall.

"Do you have a lot of homework?" Mila asked with her mouth stuffed with cookies.

"Yeah, but I don't want to talk about that. Listen, I'm going to the kingdom on Saturday," I blurted in a whisper, "and I need you to cover for me."

"Maddie!"

"Shhh!" I warned. "Whisper, because I don't want your mom to hear."

"She can't hear you, she's in the den in the back. But Maddie, you're crazy! You can't just go to this kingdom."

"Yes, I can, and it's all done. I got a ticket online like I've seen my dad do before, and I used my mom's miles. And she won't even notice because she never checks her account. And both she and my dad are going to be away. Which is why I need you to cover for me. I'm gonna tell Linda that I'm sleeping over."

"How am I supposed to cover for you, Maddie? You know I can't lie." Mila was uncomfortable doing anything sneaky. She was right; she was incapable of telling a lie. But still, she was my only hope, and I needed her.

"Listen, you don't have to do anything. Just lie low and don't say anything to anyone. Only you and Mikey know I'll be gone. Linda will think I'm here, and she won't check until Sunday night. By then, I'll be safely in the kingdom. You can then tell her you don't know anything. Because other than telling you I'm going to the kingdom, I'm not going to give you any details. That way you can honestly say you don't know anything more. Okay?"

"No, not okay at all! I have a really bad feeling about this, Maddie. But you're not going to listen to me, are you?"

"Nope," I said rather smugly, satisfied that this was one of my better schemes. "Don't worry," I assured Mila. "I completely know what I'm doing, and it's going to be fine, and Sayara and I will help Themi!"

"I don't know, Maddie …" Mila was not convinced.

Chapter 7

I was finally settling into my seat and unfastening my seat belt as we were thirty thousand feet in the air, cruising toward the kingdom.

What a week it had been getting on this flight! Buying the airline ticket had been easy with Mom's miles. I had to tell a white lie to Dad and Mom to get them to sign the international form to be able to fly as a minor. They thought it was for the school trip to Mexico the following month.

Still, I wasn't sure I would make it. But thank goodness for loyal Mila. It took me a while to convince her to fake a sleepover, but she finally agreed. I think she couldn't bear the thought of Themi facing more prison time and harsh punishment. Mila's actually a complete softie. She can't stand the thought of anyone in pain or fear. Not just anyone, but anything. Her dad had to warn her against bringing home any more stray puppies, but he always gives in to her. Luckily, their grandmother has a horse farm and is always happy to take in the strays. Mila is definitely the most sympathetic of the three of us muskies.

I clued Mikey in too, and he was tougher to manage. He wanted to come, but he would have made it all harder. I felt I could sneak around easier on my own, and besides, there was no easy way to fake a sleepover with him.

I knew that Mila would get in a lot of trouble with her mom, but I promised myself I'd make it up to her somehow. Besides, no one can stay mad at Mila very long, and her mom always forgives her. I felt kind of guilty for all the sneaking I had to do, and I knew I'd take the rap when I got back. That's the hard thing, isn't it? Sometimes you have to do something that's considered technically wrong to fix an even bigger and more outrageous wrong. Do two wrongs really make a right? Just like what Ms. Collins said in chem class, two negatives cancel to make a positive. I sure hoped Dad would see it that way, but I couldn't think about that right now—first I would need to find Sayara when we landed ...

Just as I was getting lost in my mind plotting how I would save Themi, a little hand grabbed the top of my hair. "Ouch!"

I turned with a scowl, but quickly saw the most adorable little baby girl smiling at me.

"Oh, I'm sorry. Is she bothering you?" a kind voice asked from the seat behind.

"Uh, not really," I replied politely. What else are you supposed to say when a little kid pulls your hair?

"I'm sure she was. Sofia, no pulling." The mother looked at me as baby Sofia put her hands toward me. "Oh, she just likes you."

"Babies always do," I announced. I had babysat a lot, and babies always seem to like other kids—I have no idea why.

"Hi, baby," I said, reaching for her. "Can she come sit next to me? I can play with her."

"Well ..." Her hesitant eyes looked at me. "You seem like a little girl yourself."

"I'm thirteen," I declared confidently. I was a little annoyed at yet another person thinking that I was still immature.

"Oh." The mother smiled knowingly. "Her name is Sofia, and mine is Alisha," she informed me, trying to lighten the topic. "What's yours?"

"Maddie." Baby Sofia continued to grasp my two fingers with her whole hand.

"That's a lovely name. Are you traveling alone? Going to visit your family in the kingdom?" Alisha asked with curiosity at the empty seats next to me.

"Uh, uh, yeah, sorta." Oh, no, I had totally forgotten to have a fake story in place, but I could create one quickly. "Visiting my friend, actually." Hopefully that would satisfy her. "Sofia," I quickly cooed, "peekaboo!" That always distracted babies— and in this case, hopefully her mother, too. Baby Sofia giggled, and I was safely out of that awkward set of questions. Phew.

What was I going to say to people who asked where I was going? I had planned to text Sayara when I landed. She didn't know I was coming, and I couldn't risk telling her. Aunt AK always tells me it's all about judgment. Sometimes you have to wait to be asked to help, but sometimes when you see someone in need, especially a friend, you just rise to the occasion. It's tricky to know the difference, but Sayara was so sad and feeling so helpless that I knew I had to be there with her. Even just to cheer her up, although I knew I would have to do more once I got to the kingdom.

Sayara had said that Themi was under home arrest, and her father was working hard to keep her from going back to jail or facing a harsh punishment like caning. It was unbelievable that the judgment council could just do that. There were no real jury people, Sayara said, just a couple of guys in long white robes who decided whether you were guilty and what punishment you'd get.

Themi's main crime seemed to be that she was so public in her protest and that her dad was a member of the extended ruling family. That was working for and against her. It helped get her out of jail, but now some of those judgment council guys wanted to make an example out of her.

It was a little like when my sister Angie's high school senior class made protest flyers about everything that was wrong with the school administration. It was supposed to be their senior prank, and they papered every surface in the school lobby! But Aunt AK said it touched a nerve the way it made some of the school folks look bad and incompetent, so the whole grade got detention. Angie cried that it would go on her perfect transcript and make her look bad. I thought that was so silly and wished I had been one of the people to make the flyers in the first place! Aunt AK tried to get Angie to realize that the kids who wrote all those things that the school officials were doing wrong were courageous and that Angie should want to be part of the spirit, but that just made Angie angrier. Angie has to always look perfect, and she really doesn't care about other people that much.

Somehow I just knew that Sayara would come and get me if I was at the airport. She couldn't talk me out of coming because by then, I would already be in the kingdom.

Alisha handed Sofia over the seat, and she sat happily down in the seat next to me. Chubby with a face full of smiles, Sofia came equipped with her own books, a mix of my old favorites: *Sleeping Beauty, Thomas the Tank Engine, Clifford the Big Red Dog,* and *The Cat in the Hat* by Dr. Seuss. Seeing the titles made me think of when I was little. I would make Linda read the same books over and over again. It was fun to have these books in my lap, and I cheerfully started reading to Sofia.

Alisha slid into the aisle seat a little later with some food. I hadn't fully realized how tall and beautiful she was. Her dark, gentle eyes seemed much older than her trendy jeans. I came to learn that she and her husband, Matin, who was fast asleep in the row behind me, grew up in the kingdom, but now lived in Springfield. Alisha was a pediatrician, a kids' doctor, and Matin was a civil engineer who built bridges.

"We love visiting our families, but living in the kingdom is not easy for people like us," Alisha explained.

"People like you?" What did that mean?

"What I mean is that as a woman I want to go to work and do whatever I want, and Matin wants the same for me, and now for our baby Sofia. I was raised to study and work hard. And it's not so easy to be an independent woman in the kingdom. I want to be able to drive and wear what I want, but most importantly say and think what I believe in."

There was that driving issue again. "Why can't you drive?" Maybe she had the answer.

"There's really no clear reason or even a rule. The FP, that's our faith police, says that women can't, but there's no real reason. We're the only kingdom where that's still the rule. Men can drive freely, just not women. But I didn't leave because of the driving—it's really much more. It's about being able to live freely." Sofia climbed into her lap and began to eat grapes from a bag. "I was independent, and I wanted to practice medicine and be treated as an equal at work and at home. And then I met Matin, and he was just amazing. Just look at him, he's still so cute," she whispered sweetly as she glanced back through the gap in the two seats at her sleeping husband. "Plus, he wasn't like any of the guys I grew up with. He was nice, kind, funny, and treated me as an equal. He liked hearing my opinions. He didn't act like the other guys who always thought they knew everything or that they were better than me just because they were guys. I remember once when …"

Chapter 8

A deep, commanding voice woke me from my long, blissful nap, which was more like an overnight sleep. I must have dozed off listening to Alisha. I only remembered hearing her soothing voice floating me through tales of her life with Matin, her parents, and Sofia.

The pilot announced that he would be making the descent. The long thirteen-hour flight was almost over, and I was starting to get excited and anxious thinking of what lay ahead for me.

I saw the bathroom door open and a woman emerged dressed in a full black tentlike cape with a veil covering her face.

"Hi, Maddie, sleepyhead, you're awake finally." A voice from within the tent spoke to me. I rubbed my eyes, confused.

"Maddie, it's me, Alisha. You're looking at me so weird. I'm just wearing the mandatory tent," she said as she pulled back the veil.

Mandatory? My mind was a blur. Sayara didn't wear a tent. "Sorry, Alisha, I didn't realize that you *had to* wear a tent," I stuttered. It was my first realization that this adventure was going to be very different, and perhaps I was not as prepared as I thought. I was planning to just surprise Sayara, but I didn't know where she lived or how to get there. I didn't even have a black tent to wear! I had forgotten that Sayara had mentioned the tents and how much her cousin Themi disliked them. I knew that in other countries women and men, for that matter, wore different kinds of clothes, but I hadn't realized that in the kingdom the dress code was required.

"You're at an age where you're required to wear a tent. Do you want to borrow one?" Alisha asked sweetly.

"Uh, yes, please." I was a little worried. "Will they arrest me if I don't wear one?"

Alisha smiled. "No, not at the airport, but beyond that, yes, it's always better to wear one. Don't be frightened, Maddie. My country can seem like a strange place with odd rules, but I'll take care of you until you're with your friend. Women are just required to wear some version of the tent. It's great on days when you've had too much to eat!" Alisha laughed unconvincingly. "But seriously, if you don't, the faith police can stop you and make life difficult, so it's just easier to wear the tent and veil. There's a slot over your eyes for you to see out of."

Covered in my own black tent and ready for landing, I wondered why there was a rule for women to wear heavy black tents. "You don't have a choice, Alisha?" I asked, although by now, I had guessed the answer.

Alisha sighed. "No, no choices here, Maddie. I'll be honest, I actually hate wearing one on a regular basis. Matin hates it too, and it's one reason we left the kingdom. But wearing it for a week so I can see my family is okay. I don't have a problem if some women want to wear it, but I think a woman should have the choice to decide for herself with no pressure from the faith police or her family. And there should be no consequences for not wearing it. Choice is only a choice if you can freely choose either side of anything. Right? Right."

Where had I heard that kind of thinking? Aunt AK! She always says everything in life is a choice, but real choice means that you're able to choose either side, not just one side.

After the plane landed, Alisha continued with a serious sadness in her voice. "The FP doesn't want women to be treated as equal or even feel equal, so they make all sorts of rules.

They say that this has been the way for years. But that's not completely true, and besides, just because they did it in the past doesn't make it right for now. It just makes it an old tradition that is now wrong. I hate it. The tent is just a symbol of so many unfair rules that make me feel invisible—unseen and unheard. Women should be able to wear normal clothes whenever they want, like guys. I love my country, my family, and my people. But the faith police make it hard for people to live regular lives."

"How do you know who the faith police are?" I asked as we entered the secure customs and passport control area in the arrivals terminal. It was gleaming, shiny, and modern, much more impressive than I had expected.

Alisha motioned with her eyes, although she was careful not to gesture. "Don't turn your head," she warned, "but it's the two big, angry-looking guys by the wall next to the skinny, short policeman. In the kingdom, the FP decides everything— the rules and how to enforce them. The police have no real power."

"Yeah, you can kinda tell. The two FPs look like three-hundred-pound linebackers next to the meek, skinny policeman. Any women in the faith police?" I asked, almost sure of the answer.

"Nope. The FP like to keep their little club to themselves. All guys."

The two FPs had stern faces with long, bushy beards and eyes hidden behind dark, shiny sunglasses, even though they were indoors, and they were judging everyone who walked by. They were trying to look mean and cool, but they weren't impressive to me. They looked like a bunch of middle-school bullies, randomly deciding whose lunch tray they would flip over.

"So if someone wanted to change the rules, they would have to talk to the FP, not to the king?" I asked, realizing that maybe

I had to refocus my target if I was going to help Sayara and her cousin Themi.

Alisha's eyebrows went up in concern. "Maddie, no one asks for the rules to be changed, not even the king. He actually depends on the FP more than he cares to admit. Only the grand master of the faith police can decide what to change and when. As girls, we could go to jail just for trying to talk to them, let alone asking to change the rules! Don't ever even think about it!"

Oh, boy. This place seemed to love their rules and their jails. It was gonna take some effort to get around the FP. It was a little like at school when that one temporary principal—Mr. Mean Eyes, as we all called him—decided that there would be no recess or free periods because he thought all of us kids were a bunch of goof-offs. It was the worst six months of fifth grade, but then he was transferred to another school and we got recess again.

Before I could finish my thought, Alisha, like a warm big sister, fixed my veil and tent, which was falling off my head. It was a huge tent, although I guess if you're having a bad hair day, no one really would know! Alisha laughed nervously when I told her how I felt.

"That's what my grandmother calls the silver linings in life, making light of a bad situation. You may not have to worry about your hair or how you look. But I still resent that there are no choices for women in the kingdom. It's hard to play sports or run in these ridiculous tents. We have to wear a tent every day, all the time we're in public. No choice. It's one reason that Matin and I chose to stay in Springfield. We miss our families very much, but the life here for a woman is too limiting. We want Sofia to have more choices to be everything she can be. It's not so bad to follow these outdated rules for a week or two when I'm on holiday, but all year round—I cannot do that any-more," Alisha said sadly.

Baby Sofia leaned in and hugged her gently, and she added, "And I cannot stand by and let her be any less than what she wants to be. She has the right to live a full life of choices, just like my parents let me make, especially by leaving the kingdom to go to university. There is no life here for a girl."

I had only known her for a plane ride, but I felt a kinship with Alisha, more than I did with my own real big sister. Angie would never have understood or cared. Angie wasn't a bad person, she was just all about her. She'd only care about fitting in, making sure she was wearing and doing what everyone else was. Aunt AK said Angie was living her life on autopilot, a little like Mom. Not really thinking or questioning something, especially when it didn't make sense.

Angie's biggest concerns would probably be, like, what colors the tent came in and what she got to wear underneath. Although she'd make sure to choose something other than polyester and wool, both itchy fabrics in hot weather! But as long as Angie could have her designer jeans and hip boots, she would be happy. And she'd probably choose to wear a dark green tent, which would go better with her brown hair and hazel eyes. And somehow, she'd make sure her hair would always look fabulous, no matter the tent sitting on top of it. I'd soon see many "Angies" in the kingdom, living life on autopilot, fearful of questioning unfair rules.

Waiting by the luggage carousel, I texted Sayara. Nothing. By now, my tent was feeling stuffy and airless. I had texted Sayara a bunch of times since the plane landed and hadn't received a single response. So unlike her. I was getting anxious, and maybe my nervousness was showing.

Standing in the passport check line, I hadn't seen him coming. But suddenly, I was confronted head-on by a fat, burly, mustachioed man looming at least a foot over me. He wore khaki pants that were too tight with a matching khaki shirt, like a cop with the wrong color uniform.

"Passport," his thick voice commanded, a baton in his left hand just swinging from side to side, waiting for the first misbehaving person.

Uh, hello, how about *please* and some politeness, I thought. But eager to be friendly and cooperative, I shot him a big, toothy, braces-filled smile, which I forgot was completely hidden behind the dark veil, and handed him my passport. Never having encountered creepy dudes, it didn't dawn on me to fear him, foolishly so.

"Where is your sponsor? Where is your man?" he demanded, pushing out his chest and his fat belly in a display of overweight physical presence and mediocre power.

He was definitely not having a nice day. But I was determined to brighten it for him. I kept smiling. What a weird question, I thought. "No, I don't have a man." I was still unclear why someone my age would have a man.

"Sponsor? Who is sponsor?" he demanded again.

"Sponsor? I ..." Clearly I didn't have whatever he was looking for.

"No man, no sponsor, no entry," he barked loudly. "Holding, take her to holding," he commanded the smaller, skinny policeman standing next to him.

"Holding? I'm not going anywhere but through passport control," I said defiantly. This guy was definitely not nice, and now I could feel the mean, cold lasers shooting from his shifty eyes. But I was determined not to budge.

Suddenly a voice piped up from my right shoulder. "So sorry, Captain, she is with me. The girl is with me." Matin's voice repeated the statement in case there was any confusion. They were speaking to each other past me. I was just the voiceless, faceless black blob standing in between them.

"She is with you?" the captain quizzed disbelievingly. "You are her sponsor? Why is she not then standing with you? Who is she to you?"

Matin blinked for a moment, unsure what to say. "She is our au pair." His desperate eyes looked at me silently, pleading with me to go along with him. His arms waved over Alisha and Sofia as if to prove there was both a family and a child in need of an au pair.

Au pair! I was old enough to babysit on Friday nights, but not to be a full-time nanny for a baby. However, at that moment, I gratefully realized that something more serious was underway, and I needed to play along. I nodded my head, not wanting to actually tell a lie, but knowing that I needed to be careful.

The burly, mean captain looked at us both, grunted, and then seemed satisfied.

"Make sure she follows the rules," he instructed Matin. "It will be bad for you both if she does not."

"Yes, she will be fine with us," Matin reassuringly said, gently guiding me closer with his hand toward Alisha, who had surprisingly said absolutely nothing. Her head was bowed down, and she hugged Sofia closely.

With the mean-eyed captain moving on to his next victim, I let out a huge sigh of relief, as did Alisha and Matin.

"Maddie, you have to be careful. I didn't think to check on which line you were in, and I assumed your friend had sent a sponsor to pick you up. They usually stand just behind the passport control. But when Matin saw the FP captain yelling at you, he came dashing over. Are you okay?" Alisha's words tumbled out of her mouth. Her arm was around my shoulder protectively.

"Yeah, I'm okay. But he was so not nice! What gives?" This was not at all what I had expected.

"Maddie, here in the kingdom, without a guy relative like your dad or brother, or a male sponsor waiting to receive you outside of the passport control area, you can't actually enter the country," Alisha informed me a little sheepishly.

"What? I need to have some guy meet me after passport control in order to be able to get into the country?" This place had some crazy rules. Oddly, my mind jumped to my little brother. "You mean my nine-year-old brother Jason would rank over me, just because he's a boy?" The thought horrified me, and thank goodness Jason would never find out, because he'd forever try to use it against me.

"Uh, yeah, sorry, Maddie—just another burdensome rule in the kingdom, really with no basis. But everyone just accepts it because that's how it's always been done," Alisha said.

"It seems really weird that people, especially women, would just accept this without trying to change it." I couldn't imagine people not arguing to change the rules when they were unfair. "What about their families—don't parents want to change the rules for their kids?" I was truly confused.

"I know, Maddie, I often wonder the same thing. People here have this outdated idea that women need protection, but the rest of the world has finally realized that it's not true, and now we all know that girls and boys are equal. But here in the kingdom, it's very complicated. We'll talk about it later. First, let's get out of here. Let's give Matin your passport so he can whisk all three of us 'weak' girls through." Alisha rolled her eyes and overemphasized the word *weak* to show how ridiculous she also thought the rules were.

"Okay, you two, quit clowning around. You're gonna get me in trouble. That was enough of a close call for one day," Matin said, feigning sternness.

"Oh, please, you're a guy. You so rank in the kingdom," Alisha teased him.

"Yeah, I may rank over you, but I'm just a regular guy to the FP, and they'll bust me for something. Maybe they'll say my face is not shaven enough or my jeans are too tight."

"Really, Matin?" I couldn't believe all the rules in this strange place!

"Yes, Maddie, even the guys have to follow random, strict rules. It's the only way the FP can control us all, by making us afraid of them and their overbearing rules. Now, hush. I'm sure there's some eavesdropping going on in this terminal and they can hear everything we're saying! Let's get our bags and go home," whispered Matin.

There were no questions once Matin acted as my male guardian, and we went easily through customs. I was surprised how much easier it was to be a guy in the kingdom.

Once through, I became keenly aware that Sayara had not texted me back. Maybe she wasn't in the kingdom—but even then she'd still text me back. Maybe something terrible had happened to her, too. Maybe she had been jailed for some strange reason. This was a place of weird rules, and it seemed like girls had no power. My eyes must have confessed the knot of fear that was growing inside me. I hadn't really thought about what I'd do if Sayara wasn't here.

"If you'd like, we can drop you at your friend's home," Alisha gently offered again. "Maddie?" She waved her hands in front of my eyes, trying to get my attention.

"Uh, that's very kind of you, Alisha. But I guess I'll just take car service." I had done that once when I had come home from camp and no one could pick me up at the airport.

Alisha's eyes looked down for a moment. I think she felt embarrassed for me and maybe a little for herself. "Maddie, it's not like home. You can't leave the airport alone or go in a taxi alone. No girls can."

I could feel tears welling in my eyes. I was a gazillion miles from home, on an adventure that was quickly getting out of hand. I felt Alisha's arm around my shoulder. "Maddie, it's okay. I promise you're safe with me. Come home with us, and then you can tell me what's really going on and what you're doing here." She had already figured out that I was holding a deep secret, and her kindness was relieving my fears. I wondered if all the normal people in the kingdom were just as kind. We had just met, but I knew I could trust her. All I could manage to do was nod my head yes. But I knew I would eventually have to tell her why I was here.

Chapter 9

Through the tinted windows of the black sedan, I got my first glimpse of the shiny, modern buildings. I hadn't known quite what to expect, but the kingdom seemed much more modern, at least in architecture, than I was expecting. It all looked sorta normal to me—tall window-filled skyscrapers, wide highways, cars everywhere. So it was clear to me that lots of people get to drive in the kingdom, but just not women! I tried to look inside the car windows, just in case, to see if I could find a woman driver, but nope, I couldn't see even one. Only women as passengers.

We were heading to Alisha's parents' house, driven by her childhood driver, Amar. I was surprised to see that Alisha had grown up with a driver. Alisha was quick to point out that her family wasn't rich, but they had a little money. Her father was a professor at the university, and her mother was a doctor. A driver was necessary for her mom to be able to go to the medical center, the hospital, and sometimes to patients' houses. I squirmed at the limitations of not being able to do your job properly just because of some stupid driving law. Amar had been with the family for twenty years and seemed like a kind uncle to Alisha more than anything, and it was clear that she treated him with love and respect.

While Alisha was happily distracted catching up with him in a language I didn't understand, I took a deep breath to assess all that had unfolded in the past twenty-four hours. I had snuck out of Mila's house and boarded a flight to the kingdom, all along fooling everyone that I was visiting a friend. But had I been

fooling myself? My plan had hit a wall. Not being able to connect with Sayara was not part of my plan. How would I find her
address? But how could I even go there since I couldn't seem to
go anywhere by myself? I was going to have to confess to Alisha.
The thought was unnerving, and I hoped she wouldn't call my
parents. I'd be shipped back on the first flight and wouldn't be
able to help Themi and Sayara, the whole reason I was here. I
would have to find a way to convince Alisha to give me help and
most importantly, some time.

Forty-five minutes after careening through congested
highways and rich and poor neighborhoods, we arrived in
front of an old but well-preserved house. Beige walls formed
the edges of the compound, and inside there was a large main
house and a smaller cottage, which Alisha said was for Amar
and his wife, who helped out in the house. They had no children and so Alisha, an only daughter, was the light of their
life, too.

Before I could say a word, a gray-haired older man in jeans
and a blue plaid shirt came running out of the house, followed
by a woman wearing a beautiful, flowing caftan with a burgundy print. Her long hair was streaked gray and black, and she
wore a beaming smile.

Alisha ran to embrace them both. Minutes later, after lots
of tight hugging, laughing, and some tears, Alisha turned to me
and motioned for me to approach.

"Mom and Dad, this is Maddie, my new friend. She's with
us for a short while."

Alisha's mom stepped forward and gave me an unexpected
tight hug. "Welcome, Maddie. Welcome to our home." I was not
expecting this warmth and felt relieved and happy. "My name
is Danah, and you can call me Grandma Danah. Now where is
my little baby Sofia?" And with that, she turned to gently take
the sleeping baby from Matin's arms, cooing softly so as not to

wake her. Whispering, she motioned her chin toward Alisha's father. "And this is Grandpa Mansur."

"Welcome, Maddie. You must all be tired. Come," he directed. "You can freshen up, and we have plenty of food waiting. I want to hear all about your journey."

An hour later, showered and wearing jeans and a T-shirt, I joined the family in the living room, a spacious, warm room lined with books and a few paintings. In the center, a cushy-looking, brown *U*-shaped sofa surrounded a marble table filled with food. I could see where Alisha got her generosity—plates filled with meat pies, kebabs, bread, hummus, tabbouleh, cookies, fruits, and more were spread everywhere. Baby Sofia was now awake eating grapes and playing with some blocks next to Grandma Danah, who was happily sitting cross-legged on the floor. When Sofia saw me, she waddled over, and everyone turned toward me with big smiles. It was as welcoming as Mila's home, full of generosity and kindness. It also reminded me of what my family home lacked, warmth and welcome.

One wall was full of books and photos. Alisha explained, "My dad is a history professor at the university and loves reading about astronomy and philosophy, too. And my other inspiration in life is my mom, who is also a pediatrician." Hugging her, she added that her mom could speak three languages fluently. Gratefully English was one of them. Education and self-betterment were part of Alisha's family motto. Just like in my dad's family, especially with Grammy and Gramps.

Grammy has deteriorated over the years and is now confined to a wheelchair because of a rare muscle disease. Her disease hasn't been easy, but Grammy has too much spunk to let anything or anyone keep her down. She and Gramps live next door. Dad insists on taking good care of his parents even though they sometimes drive him crazy! Well, mainly Grammy drives everyone crazy. But I'm her favorite, if one can call it that. Grammy is demanding and tough on everyone, including me. Laziness is not permitted, and half-efforts are never tolerated. Grammy says that I give her the most hope. Angie is too much like my mom and Grammy doesn't like her, although she's too polite to say so directly to me. I overheard her tell Aunt AK that she thinks my mom is too lazy and neglects us kids. Grammy had been against my dad marrying my mom, but he went ahead anyhow. In a weird way, I'm glad he did, or I wouldn't exist!

Grammy became a doctor but said she would have joined the army if she could have. But women weren't allowed in the military back then. Sometimes I forget that even back home, it wasn't too many years ago that women couldn't do much. Now, I have all the choices that I want. Grammy says sometimes that's dangerous. "When you have all the choices in the world, you take them for granted and don't work hard enough for any of them," she'd lecture me. "Study hard, work hard, and do something useful with your life." That's how Grammy evaluates all of us, Dad and Aunt AK included—by how hard we work and if we're doing something useful. "Everyone in your generation wants the latest phone, but no one's thinking of how to buy them," she'd moan. "When I was little, we didn't dare ask for something unless we knew how we would pay for it, and even then you just didn't ask for stuff you didn't need." Grammy came over on a boat with her parents, who were poor but hardworking. It defines her still. Sometimes, a little too much! But I love her nonetheless. Dad says that he doesn't always agree with her, but he loves her spitfire courage. And while Grammy is a bulldog, Gramps is the gentle spirit. They are a perfect yin-yang balance to each other. He was an architect and keeps us laughing with his jokes and cartoons. He's funny, easygoing, and very wise. They're a balanced match, and I can't imagine them any other way.

My thoughts of home were interrupted by Alisha's retelling of the airport scene.

"It was really stupid, Mom, the FP almost didn't let Maddie in because she didn't have a man with her."

"Yes, I was wondering how you got through airport controls. And the tent, Maddie, where did you get that?" Grandma Danah asked me.

But before I could respond, Alisha interrupted. "I had an extra one, Mom, and quite luckily because the FP guy was in a really bad mood today."

"He must have had a bad lunch," Grandpa Mansur piped in, making us all laugh. "These guys think they're so tough and righteous, but they're nothing but regular people abusing the laws. In my day, when I was younger, both the laws and rulers were sensible. And there was no ridiculous FP!"

"I know," Grandma Danah wistfully sighed. "The sensible old days, when the FP didn't make women wear tents. We could do anything we wanted. We dressed as we wanted. I loved wearing my suits, the skirts and jackets. Made me feel professional, not like a lumpy potato sack. Never take a right for granted, because it can always be taken away from you! We regular people didn't see the dangers of the FP until it was too late and we had lost all our freedoms. Once upon a time, we could all do whatever we wanted, even drive! And now look at what we've become. A land where only the rich and the FP have power. The rest of us, we don't matter anymore."

My ears perked up when she mentioned the freedoms of long ago. "Really, you could drive back then?"

"Yes, dear Maddie. We could do anything. Well, of course, most of us didn't have cars back then, as they were very expensive. But there were no rules that prohibited driving or forced women to hide under black tents or in their houses to avoid being seen by men and outsiders. We were normal and free. We went to university, to the store, to work, wherever. Our families taught us to study hard, work hard. Women were still just starting to get opportunities, but we had the feeling that we could do anything if we just tried. It was a bit like where you live now, Maddie. It's how I got to go to medical school and start my practice. But now, it's all gone backward. It's too hard for girls now. There are barriers everywhere."

"What happened?" If there weren't stupid rules not so long ago, then it wouldn't be so hard to get rid of them.

Grandpa Mansur dived headfirst into the subject. "Well, little Maddie," he began, clearing his throat, "the current FP took over when the king's father was dying slowly of cancer, forty years ago. They just wanted power over people and used the king's weakness to seize it. Throughout history, people everywhere have always grabbed power, and not always for good reasons. Of course, they pretended that they were protecting the faith, but it was never clear whose version of the faith. After a year, there were many new rules forbidding lots of things, especially for women and people outside of the faith. If they wanted us to live like people did a thousand years ago, they should have just given us horses and huts. Instead, they let people have free things like houses and healthcare, but made really strict, stupid rules. People were willing to listen and sacrifice their freedoms because they wanted the money and an easy life. Greed can lead to a terrible fate."

Grandpa Mansur snorted in anger at various points in his story, but he continued with a sense of new urgency to make sure I knew the real version. "Now, Maddie," he said, looking right at me to make sure I was listening. And I was! "People here have lost their way. The free stuff was paid for by oil, and it has blinded them to the values that our forefathers taught us— honor, decency, respect, and kindness for one another. Now a little money is dangled and people sell their souls, forgetting that freedoms are more important than having fancy cars or houses."

That sounded just like what Grammy always said: "Money can corrupt the soul. People who don't know their purpose in life let money and the things money can buy become their purpose."

Grammy believes that working hard and making lots and lots of money is important and just fine, especially like my dad or Aunt AK has done, but so long as it doesn't make people lazy and indulgent. Sometimes Grammy is over the top in wanting us to be hardworking, like when she wakes us up at seven o'clock even on the weekends to do our chores. I don't mind the chores, but seven o'clock in the morning, yuck. I kinda get why she does it. But she makes sure our dad and Linda give us chores. She tells my dad that she will be the first to box our ears—and his—and string us up by our toes if we become disrespectful or rude. And knowing Grammy, I really think she would!

My thoughts of Grammy were interrupted by Grandma Danah's knowing voice, which brought me back to the conversation. "And now the regular people suffer as the money from oil is drying up, and people realize that only the royals live comfortably and freely." She sighed and continued, "Only the royals are safe from the FP. They have a pact between them to not bother each other and let each one do their own thing. Royals can do whatever they want inside their houses while the rest of us live in fear that at any time, any day, there could be a random knock on the door from the FP making sure we are obeying all their rules. It's not about the faith, it's about their power and money." Her voice was heavy.

She went on, bouncing baby Sofia on her lap, stroking her hair. "It's why we told Alisha and Matin to leave and live somewhere where they could be free and have lots of opportunity.

I miss them." A tear fell down Grandma Danah's cheek, and in that same instant, Alisha was kneeling beside her mom, hugging.

"We miss you too, Mom. You can come and live with us anytime."

"That we know, but this is the land of our ancestors, our home, our kingdom. No matter what the FP has done to destroy the old ways of life, we cannot leave. We are happiest here with our large family and friends, even if the society has changed. There are two sets of rules here, one for the rich royals and another for regular people like us."

Grandpa Mansur chimed in, "And what's worse, the king is king by birth, not by accomplishment. He and all his royal brothers were spoiled little boys who have grown up into spoiled big boys, caring for no one other than themselves, not really working. Idle hands and minds make for mischief."

I laughed when I heard that expression and quickly had to explain to surprised faces that it was exactly what my grand-mother always said. I mimicked Grammy: "Be useful, do something meaningful with your life, Maddie."

Grandma Danah smiled and tipped her head at me. "That Grammy of yours must be very wise—I would like to meet her one day. Women like your grandmother and my mother, in our day, we appreciated the changes in society and the opportuni-ties that came to us as a result."

"Mom, no lecturing," Alisha gently advised. She looked at me apologetically. "My mother gets carried away with the poli-tics in the kingdom and starts lecturing ..." But I didn't mind. It was like being at home.

"It's not lecturing to have an opinion!" Grandma Danah said indignantly. "In my day, we were raised to value working hard, getting a good education, being sensible, and showing respect to our elders and family. Now everyone is just a bling addict.

Buying flashy, expensive stuff they don't need or even often want except for thinking it makes them cooler. Everyone just wants to keep up with whatever everyone else has or does—they don't think for themselves."

"No, that's not lecturing," Alisha said sarcastically, smiling at me and rolling her eyes.

"Oh, Alisha," Grandma Danah said, exasperated, "just wait until Sofia gets older and treats you as if you're an opinionated old dinosaur." I could tell she was just pretending that her feelings were hurt. She hugged Alisha and playfully winked at me.

Alisha said, "I respect you and you're only half a dinosaur, but times are changing, Mom."

"And change is fine. I'm online, hip with your music. But some changes like laziness and stupidity—and just buying a ton of shiny stuff for no good reason—these are the kinds of changes that are no good for any of us, nor for our kingdom."

Alisha rolled her eyes again, but to me it was like listening to Grammy and Gramps, who at that moment, I missed very much.

"That's okay, my grandfather says the same things," I said. "He thinks he's hip by opening up the sunroof when he drives. He sends me all these whack video links, and most of them have viruses, but I haven't the heart to tell him, so I just delete 'em. He's more fun when he thinks he's cool, especially when he gets on the dance floor at a family party. Everyone thinks he's adorable, waving his hands above his head and shaking his body, sometimes even out of rhythm. He's a gentle soul with a fun spirit, which I love."

Our conversation covered many topics over the next two hours. Sitting cozy on a large cushion on the floor, I instinctively felt like this was my family and I had been part of them from the beginning of my life. Warm food was periodically added to my small plate, and I devoured it all. As Grandma Danah spooned some warm cakes on my plate and refilled my milk, she noted, "Faith is a little like comfort food, is it not? We are born into it and assume ours to be the best, the tastiest—but in fact, everyone thinks their home food is the best. It's what we know first and what we have enjoyed. But what if you were born in a different kingdom with different comfort food and a different faith, wouldn't you then think that was best?"

It certainly seemed sensible to me. I'd be rooting for the kingdom with cakes and ice cream as comfort food.

"People in the kingdom have forgotten to think for themselves. We are sheep," added Grandpa Mansur. "We do whatever we are told, without thinking through whether it's rational or reasonable. Let's not confuse unity with uniformity. We need to be happy about what brings us together as well as what makes us unique, in how we look and think and act. Who wants to live in a place where everyone looks and acts the same? How boring!"

"Mansur," Grandma Danah interrupted, "you're right, but it's also our own fault that we don't teach our children to think for themselves. We reward them for being obedient, not for being creative or thinking critically." Her hand rested on his back. "We have created our own mess, and now we don't know how to fix it." He leaned back into her. They were in sync not just as a married couple, but in thought and spirit. It was the same electric, loving connection I had seen with Gramps and Grammy.

On the plane, Alisha had told me of her parents' love story. It had started when they first met in the university.

"Not surprisingly," Grandpa Mansur said with a twinkle in his eye, "Grandma Danah was a ball of spitfire full of opinions who advocated for the poorest and sickest. I fell in love with her at first sight. Full of energy and full of compassion. That's what I wanted in my life partner, someone with the brains, heart, and energy to face life with humor and kindness. She is also relentless when she puts her mind to something. Watch out!"

Alisha had told me that it was her parents' marriage that made her look for a man she could love and respect. Her parents were very much twin halves joined in the adventure of life. So when she met Matin, it was also love at first sight. I inhaled the love and emotion, loving every drop of it. I felt like I could have been Grandma Danah's daughter, too.

I soon came to find out that Grandpa Mansur was as frustrated with the FP as Alisha and I were. "The FP now runs the schools and decides what kids should learn. This is ridiculous. Can you imagine just ignoring science or facts when you don't like them?" Grandpa Mansur's eyes popped from his head as his arms flailed in anger. He was on a roll, and there was no stopping him.

"Misinformation, that's what happens. The FP changes history and science to suit their own logic. You can't just change the past to fit your own crazy way of seeing the world. Things happened—wars, ideas, events, scientific discoveries—and it's important you young ones learn it all accurately, not just some half-baked, cockamamy version that a bunch of fake-believers think you should learn. They're even rewriting the textbooks. Can you believe that, Alisha? My goodness, I'd like to give 'em a piece of my mind direct to their face!" His face was angry, and his fists were raised. He looked ready to take on the first FP dude in sight. "People in our kingdom have forgotten our real history. They go to schools where faith has decided what they should learn, not science or philosophy, and so they never learn how to think. You can have information, but that doesn't mean you have knowledge. Education is important—but the right kind of education. If you can't think for yourself and make good decisions, what use is it?" His breathless voice conveyed the urgency of his words.

"Mansur, calm down, your blood pressure … remember your heart condition," Grandma Danah cautioned him.

"Forget my darn heart! The grand master of the FP is going to give me a heart attack. He didn't even go to a proper university. Imagine going to a cooking school and then acting like a doctor—garbage is all that comes out! You know, Maddie, faith schools—of any faith—are afraid of change. Our FP has had the most dangerous effect on our kingdom. They enforce harsh rules against girls, put wrong ideas in the heads of boys and girls, and bully everyone with fear and strict punishments into doing what they want publicly, just so they can keep their total control and power." His words tumbled from his mouth as he gave me a fast lesson in all that was wrong with the FP. As if the airport hadn't already given me that!

"They hate questions and only want blind obedience, but that's not learning. The FP is afraid of questions. How ridiculous! What intelligent person is afraid of questions?" he demanded. "Only weak people who don't know what they're doing are afraid. You don't have to have the answers, but you can't be afraid of the questions. Real faith is about following what's in our hearts, not what the FP commands. Our royals don't care about the people, but they're too afraid of the FP to challenge them. The royals only care about protecting their money. And the world has allowed them to get a lot of money by wanting our oil and our beautiful resources. Do you know how beautiful the kingdom once was?" Grandpa Mansur was panting now. Small sweat beads covered the top of his forehead, and his frustration and anger were boiling over.

"You should try to change it," I said quietly.

"Change it? Change it!" He sputtered half a question and half an answer as my words seemed to deflate his energetic burst of passion. He paused, then his voice went soft. "Oh, little one, I'm old. I just can't stand by watching people destroy my kingdom. I love my country." He sighed. "Changing things is for young people like you. I just want to enjoy my grandkids and read. Young people, they are where the change should come from."

Like through Themi, I thought. She was the very brave one fighting the FP and the stupid rules, risking prison.

Alisha's soft voice gently asked the same question again, to which she already knew the answer. "Dad, why don't you and Mom come live with us? The kingdom is a mess. It's not a place for you anymore."

"You are a good daughter, but I cannot leave, and neither can your mother. Running away does not solve the problems. This is our home and the home of our ancestors. We belong here, and I love my country. I just don't love what the royals have done to it. They pretend to have faith, but in the safety of their gigantic compounds, they do everything that is banned." Deep-rooted anger shone through his eyes. His voice conveyed his disgust with the double set of rules, one for the royals and another for regular people in the kingdom. "They have taken away our freedoms and the decency of regular people and replaced it with heartless, cold, fancy skyscrapers. We are prisoners of our greed for luxury. The latest technology is just a tool, but it cannot feed your soul. As a kingdom, we are lost on our insides. The only way forward is to remember that we live together as humans with kindness and compassion. If we treated others as we want them to treat us, kindness would prevail. The royals should remember that. The culture and history of our beautiful kingdom is not the life we have now, where blind obedience is the only option. Once upon a time, we were a place of wisdom, tolerance, and richness of the spirit." There were tears in his eyes.

"Okay, time to change the subject. Mansur, I love you too much to lose you to a heart attack over those nasty FPs. Subject closed for now. That's the end of it." And that was it. No one questioned Grandma Danah, as her word was final. Her attention now shifted to me and food.

"Maddie, what else can I get you to eat?" Grandma Danah was already adding more pastries to my plate without waiting for my response. "Some milk? A growing girl needs her milk. Now, who feeds you at home?"

Ah, the dreaded change of conversation.

"Most days, Linda, my nanny, makes dinner for us. I'm too old for a nanny, but Dad says Linda is part of our family for life."

"Your father sounds like a kind man, Maddie. Who else is in your family, and who knows you are here?"

Grandma Danah did not mince words. She was direct, and it was clear that she expected honest answers. She was too smart to be tricked and too nice for me to want to fool her. I had no choice other than to tell them everything, but in my heart I knew that she—all of them—would understand. I then began confessing the whole story, starting with meeting Sayara two weeks earlier.

"… and so two weeks after I met Sayara I ran away to the kingdom, but it seems that my plan has some holes. Sayara isn't answering my calls or texts, and I don't know how to help her. But please, you can't send me back yet, because I have to help Sayara with her cousin Themi first."

There was silence. No one seemed to know what to say. I was worried that they would freak out. And then Grandma Danah's gentle words came. "Maddie, I understand all you're trying to do. You're brave, but young and naïve. The world is more unkind than you can even imagine. But you are safe here. Let Grandpa Mansur and me talk while you all go to bed. It's late." And with that, the subject was closed for the moment. The look of concern on her face spoke volumes. I knew I was safe for the time being, but I was worried about what would happen next.

Chapter 10

The vibrations of my phone woke me. It must have been hours later—or was it the next morning? I had lost track of time, and for a moment I panicked before remembering that I was safely sleeping in Alisha's house.

It was Mila. Again. She had already sent me ten desperate messages to call my dad, warning me that everyone was freaking out. I had a gazillion missed calls from my dad and just as many messages. I had been smart to turn off my location finder, and since those early texts to Sayara, I had decided not to use my phone for anything, not even to check online. I knew that everything could be tracked, and I was determined to try to stay under the radar. If Sayara texted me, I could and would respond, but otherwise, I was off the grid.

I needed to help Sayara and Themi—only then would my dad understand why I did it this way. Oh, who was I kidding? He wasn't going to understand, no way. At least I knew he wouldn't ground me. True to form, Mom had already sent me three messages, calling me selfish for ruining her week with her sisters and threatening to stop talking to me if I didn't respond right away. She said the same thing two winters ago when I crashed into a tree skiing and lost my phone in the snow, plus fractured my leg. Whatever. For my mom, the world starts and ends with my mom. She would never be able to understand why I had come to help Sayara and Themi.

Buzz. Another message, this time from Linda trying to coax me into calling her. My dad had tried the same. I really felt bad. Linda didn't deserve to be worried, and neither did my dad, but I was very torn. I wanted to let them know I was safe, and yet I needed to first make sure that Sayara and Themi were safe. I was surprised that Grandma Danah was so spunky and determined. I knew she could help me. I plugged the phone back into the charger. I wasn't going to answer, but seeing their messages made me feel just a little safer and connected to my life at home.

Coming down the elegant stairs into the open, plant-filled foyer, I could overhear Grandma Danah, Grandpa Mansur, and Alisha talking in the breakfast room facing the garden in the back of the house. I crept behind the double door as I listened in.

"Mom, she doesn't understand how much trouble she has put us all in." Alisha's concerned voice worried me. Put them in trouble? How? I wondered.

"She's a naïve but very brave young girl. She means well, Alisha. We will protect her, and don't worry about your father or me. We are old—the FP cannot do anything to us."

"Not do anything!" Alisha's whispers grew louder and more exasperated. "They can jail you, Mom, for letting her be here once it is clear that she doesn't have the proper entry papers. Maddie doesn't know what Matin had to tell the low-level FP at the airport. We're lucky that the guy could be bribed with an easy hundred!"

"Alisha's right about the FP, Danah," Grandpa Mansur said as he poured himself another cup of coffee. "It's not just us, though—it's Maddie, Alisha, Matin, even the baby. We need to get Maddie out of the kingdom before anyone wonders how we have a new girl in the house without proper registration, and we can't register her without the correct entry papers. It's a mess. Besides, what about her family? I'm sure they are looking everywhere. And it's only a matter of time before they look through airport security cameras and spot her getting on a flight to the kingdom. How did she manage to get here anyhow, Alisha?"

"She said she used her mom's miles. Her mom apparently is always traveling and never checks the account so she wouldn't notice. She's only been gone for two days, but I'm sure that they are already searching for her. Eventually they'll track her to the kingdom."

"Okay, you two, go," Grandma Danah ordered, waving them off with her hands. "Go somewhere. Maybe go to the shops. Matin already took baby Sofia and went to visit his cousin in his office. With you all gone, I can talk to Maddie without alarming her. As much as she is brave, she is still just a child."

"Okay, Mom, we'll go. Come on, Dad, I am dying to see what's new at the mall." Alisha linked her arm into her dad's and they walked through the back door to the car.

I decided I had to make my entrance, although less grandly than I normally do, given that I was reminded of how much grief I was giving my own family and now this sweet family. Entering the breakfast area, I saw that Grandma Danah was already sipping her coffee and eating some toast and juicy-looking oranges. "Come, Maddie, welcome. I cannot quite say good morning as it is almost eleven o'clock and soon the afternoon. Are you feeling rested and fresh?"

"Yes, thank you. I slept very well."

"Alisha always loved that room, tucked away from the noise and facing the garden and courtyard."

"It's beautiful," I replied a bit absentmindedly. My thoughts were elsewhere as Grandma Danah was quick to see. I had come here to help Sayara and Themi and her cause for freedom, not to create a bigger mess, and now I could only think about the danger I had brought on this kind family.

"You are thinking of something else, are you not, little Maddie? I see it in your eyes. You are wondering how to help this friend of yours and her cousin. But what about your family, Maddie? They must be very worried about you. Have they not tried to contact you?"

There was no use in lying to Grandma Danah; she was too perceptive. Plus I needed advice and help, so I told her about the many texts and missed calls, but also that I was not going back until I had contacted Sayara and seen her cousin. I also told her how sorry I was that I had put them all in danger of prison. By then, tears of frustration were pouring down my face. They had been bottled up for several days, and now with Grandma Danah, I felt relief at being able to unburden myself. She walked over to my side of the table and held me in her arms as I sobbed uncontrollably. I didn't feel so brave at that moment, just lost.

"You remind me of me, Maddie, when I was your age—full of energy, determination, and perhaps most of all, hope and optimism. I am now an old lady, and the optimism has been slowly drained from me like a leaky faucet over many years of lost hopes. I once thought I could change the minds of people who didn't share my values. Make them more tolerant, kind, and helpful. It took me a long time to realize that they had their own values that they clung to for life, and changing people is not so easy."

She paused, and I wondered if she wanted me to speed ahead in life and join her in the land of lost hopes, too.

"But, my, uh ..." she slowly continued, her voice slightly choking with emotion. "Uh, my father ... he urged me to continue on to medical school and to not give up. He'd say 'Be the best doctor you can be, Danah, and help people by taking care of their bodies. Perhaps one day their minds and souls will heal, too.' I admired his principles very much. He was a doctor to the royals, but secretly he provided free medical services to all the laborers who worked outside the palace. The royals only give medical service to people who are born in the kingdom, never to the workers brought here to build our palaces, modern buildings, and schools. Those people have nowhere to go. My father found that unconscionable, especially for a doctor, since you take an oath to help people, all people, not just rich or local people. No one knew but my mother and me. Families would bring their sick kids or elderly at night to our back door. They knew my father would never charge for being their doctor." Tears glistened in her defiant eyes. "In a way, you have reminded me that I have something left to do in this life—to help pave the way forward for others, especially for those younger and still more hopeful than me."

She paused and then looked directly at me again, but I could tell that her eyes were lost in an old world. "So, little Maddie, you want to change the world, eh?"

I could only nod my head intently, since the words were stuck in my throat. I was confused, determined, unsure, hopeful … a jumble of emotions and energy.

"Well, then," her gentle voice commanded as she cupped my chin and my eyes looked upward into her kind, wise ones, "let's start figuring out how to fix things, shall we?" I leapt into her arms. It was as if I was with my own grandmother. Grandma Danah was just like her, and she had accepted my crazy scheme and me—and here she was, hugging me. I was so happy and so sad at the same time. I really missed Grammy, Aunt AK, and Dad.

Chapter 11

Later that afternoon, as the blazing sun dipped from its mid-day peak, I was sprawled on the living room floor playing with baby Sofia. She wanted me to build a tower of wooden blocks, but every time I did, she'd knock them over. I began to realize that was the real game, the knocking over, not the building.

Grandma Danah came to the living room in an excited rush. "Maddie, I think that Mansur and I have figured out who Sayara is," she announced. "Mansur found a small article in last week's newspaper that said that eight girls were arrested for trying to drive a car. The photo of the girls being arrested is here, and one of the girls is Princess Themi!"

Princess Themi? Did that mean Sayara was royal? My mind was wandering as Alisha tapped into the conversation. "Are you sure, Mom?"

"Yes, your father is very sure. He recognized her from the university. She was in his history class her first year. She often took off the veil in class so she could be part of the class discussions and debate."

I was finally absorbing the information. "So does that mean Sayara is a princess if they're cousins?"

"Yes, Maddie, most likely." Grandpa Mansur had entered the living room with a cup of coffee. Placing it on the small table next to the brown sofa, he sat down and continued. "Maddie, our royals are actually a huge extended family. While there is only one king, his great-grandfather was the first modern king to take on the throne two hundred years ago. Since then, his great-grandfather's children went on to have many children themselves, and then so on and so on. So currently, there are about fifteen thousand people in the kingdom who claim to have royal blood, but only about two thousand of them have money and power. Themi's father is not one of the most powerful ones. He might have a lot of money, but not so much power."

"That explains why Themi could have been arrested then," said Alisha, who was listening intently. "A powerful royal would never be arrested—it makes for bad press." Her voice dripped with cynicism.

I was beginning to understand a little more, but it still wasn't clear how we could help Themi if she was already part of the royal family. "When I video-chatted with Sayara last, she said that her uncle had quickly gotten Themi out of the kingdom jail and into house arrest. What does that mean?"

"It means that she is in her house and is forbidden to leave, but at least she is not in a dirty and scary city jail," said Grandpa Mansur. "We might be able to find her more easily, then. She is likely at her family compound. The girls might both live on the same royal family compound."

I asked, "What's a royal family compound?"

"Just a gated compound with all the houses inside, but specifically for royals. There's extra security and privacy," Grandma Danah informed me.

"Actually, they're incredibly elaborate and rich with huge houses, pools, gardens, and very high walls, giving them the privacy to do whatever they want without the FP sticking their noses in their business," Matin added, walking in and rubbing his eyes after his afternoon nap.

"Sleep well, lazy bum?" Alisha asked, tousling his hair as he sat down next to her.

"Excellent. I was more tired than I realized. That's one thing I love about the kingdom and hot weather. Huge, delicious lunches and long afternoon naps! I miss that at home. We're all too busy working. We should nap more."

"Matin's right about the houses, Maddie," said Grandpa Mansur, ignoring the conversation about napping and refocusing on the royals and their misbehavior. "The royals have created a separate country for themselves inside these compounds. The guys do everything that is banned by the FP. They party, drink, play loud music, and wear whatever they want, all of which is perfectly fine to do, but it would be more fair if all of us had the same choices as they do."

"Play loud music? The FP doesn't allow that?" I asked. Every day was getting weirder as the can't-do list was growing. "Maybe it would be easier if they just told you what you *can* do, since the list is so much shorter!"

Everyone laughed, but it was more awkward than happy. I had reminded them again of their limitations.

"The FP only lets us listen to faith-based chants, no rap or pop music allowed," said Matin. "But inside the royal compounds, they do everything they want. And when they get really bored, they just go on holiday to another country where they can do anything and everything—men and women. And let me tell you, from what I have seen, they live some pretty wild lives outside of the kingdom!"

"Like drive," I said. "Now that's a wild idea."

"Maddie, you're very focused on this driving ban, aren't you?" Grandma Danah asked.

"Rightly so, she should be," Grandpa Mansur intervened. "It's symbolic of the silly rules that we accept in order to be considered good citizens and keepers of the faith. But it's not even based in faith. Driving has no bearing on faith. The FP just uses it as a way to keep women from advancing and becoming equal partners in society in the eyes of the law and our community. How can you be equal if you aren't even considered equal enough to be able to drive yourself to university or work or to the store or even a friend's house? Maddie, you are wiser than you may realize to focus on that slippery slope of freedom. It represents a great deal more than simply steering a wheel."

"Okay, Dad, I get it, and I know, I know. But now we need to focus on how to get Themi out of jail or house arrest or wherever she may be," said Alisha. "Let's focus, everyone. A girl's well-being is at stake."

I liked this no-nonsense side of Alisha.

"Well put, my daughter," Grandpa Mansur said. "I just wanted Maddie to know some of the reasons why we're in the mess we're in. But you are correct. Time for some action, enough talking."

Matin offered the first idea. "How about if Maddie, Grandma Danah, and I go to their compound and see what we can find out? Alisha, you and the baby stay with your dad in case we need you to get us out of trouble! Hopefully not, but who knows with the FP and the royals. They decide whatever crazy rules they want to enforce whenever they like. Maddie couldn't even enter the country until the man in me showed up." Matin was trying to be funny, but his face showed his concern. I was sorry that I had dragged them all into this mess.

An hour later, seated in the family car, we drove in silence to the other side of town. The streets became more tree-lined, even in the sandy desert, and the palm trees stood still with no wind to even rustle their fronds. It was hot, even more stifling than the Bahamas on a summer day!

I sat next to Matin. He only broke his pensive demeanor to remind me to not say a word, not even look up, if we were stopped by an FP, especially because it would be so clear that I was a foreigner. The FP preferred to have very few foreigners visit the kingdom, and especially not in the royals' part of town.

Most foreigners lived in foreign housing compounds and were only in the kingdom to work in approved companies. We had passed a few of those foreigner compounds already. I couldn't see much, since there were high walls lined with desert shrubs. Grandma Danah told me as we drove by that life inside was more free and people could wear what they wanted and do what they wanted to some extent, although sometimes the FP waited outside to spot-check if people were breaking any of the kingdom's many strict rules. It seemed as if the FP were just a bunch of bullies who randomly enjoyed showing off their power and harassing people.

As Amar drove our black sedan toward the gate of what seemed like a discreet entrance, I could see that the ten-foot-high walls extended down both sides of the gatehouse for what seemed like a mile. I couldn't even see the edges of the wall. Clearly this was a huge compound.

Amar jumped out of the car at the gate and started to talk to the gatekeeper. I couldn't hear what they were saying, and I wouldn't have understood it anyhow, but the gatekeeper's face and arm gesture made me realize that we were not going to be allowed in.

Amar returned to the car. "No entry, madam," he informed Grandma Danah. "The gatekeeper says no entry. Princesses are not allowed visitors."

That was telling. "Grandma Danah, he mentioned princesses, so maybe Themi and Sayara are both here!" I started to get excited.

"Slow down, Maddie. We can't go in, and we can't confirm," Matin warned.

"Matin is right, Maddie. Let's think for a moment." Grandma Danah's voice made it clear she was trying to create a plan. "Amar, please ask him *when* Sayara can have a visitor. Please make sure to use her name," she told him.

"Okay, madam." Amar left the car. There was a stern look on the gatekeeper's face, a few exchanged words, and the same no-entry gesture with a backward wave of his hand. Amar returned to the car.

"No entry," Amar said, annoyed. "Very strict gatekeeper."

"What else did he say?" Grandma Danah asked.

"He said I was very disrespectful and must call her Princess Sayara, and she, too, is not allowed visitors."

"Excellent!" Grandma Danah exclaimed. "Now we know two things: Sayara is a princess from this side of the royal family, and she lives here, too."

"Okay," said Matin, "but we still cannot see her."

"I wish we could get a message to her," I sighed out loud.

"The gatekeeper is not nice, Maddie," Amar reminded me. "Very protective and strict."

For a moment I was discouraged, but then it dawned on me. "That's it! Protective. He is protecting Sayara. Maybe he thinks we're with the FP or something. We have to convince him that we're her friends."

"Okay, but how?" asked Matin. "He's not exactly going to take our word for it."

"I know!" An idea burst into my head. Sometimes when I'm on a roll that happens. Ideas pop all over! "Amar, please tell him that I am Sayara's friend who she met in the Bahamas last week. Also tell him that I know that he taught her how to play soccer and she is an awesome goalie. Sayara told me that no one knows her gatekeeper used to teach her soccer, and her mom got furious when she found out."

"Maddie, that's very quick thinking. Amar, if he accepts that information, give him this small piece of paper with our home number." Grandma Danah quickly jotted down the home number with my name. "Tell him to secretly get it to Sayara. If she's anything like you, Maddie, she'll figure out how to call you!"

"Mom," Matin said, "are you sure we should leave our number? He might not be trustworthy and might give it to Sayara's father or the FP instead."

"Have faith, Matin," said Grandma Danah. "He looks like a decent person, and sometimes we have to have faith that people may help. He seems to be protective of Sayara, instructing Amar to call her by her 'princess' title. Let's try again."

Amar cautiously stepped out of the car once more. I could see he was not thrilled with the task we had given him. Indeed, he looked afraid. But he spoke softly to the gatekeeper again, and this time, it seemed to work. The gatekeeper peered at the car, but the black tint on the windows made it hard to see in. He looked both ways and behind him, then quickly took the paper and stuffed it in his pocket. Success! He would get a message to Sayara. I felt like we were spies working together.

Back in the car, Amar said, "Maddie, you had the secret code! Once I mentioned soccer and him teaching Sayara, he immediately softened. He didn't say much, but he said he would try."

"That's all we can hope for," said Grandma Danah. "Let's go home. Mission for this afternoon accomplished."

Chapter 12

I was sleeping soundly that night, perhaps because my belly was full from all the meat pies and chocolate cake I had eaten at dinner. Or perhaps I just felt safe with Alisha's family and relieved that we had at least found out where Sayara lived. I was more determined than ever to challenge this silly driving ban.

I was awakened by a loud ringing. Was it Sayara? A light in the hallway and a soft tapping on my door filled me with anticipation. I took the phone from Grandma Danah, who motioned for me to come to her room after I was done talking. It was Sayara.

"Sayara!" I whispered.

"Oh, Maddie, I am so happy to hear your voice!" I could feel the warmth of Sayara's kind smile. It was just like in the Bahamas.

"Yes! I've been trying to reach you, Sayara."

"So much is going on, and everyone is looking for you!"

"What do you mean, everyone is looking for me?" I was shocked. I had been looking for Sayara. Who was looking for me?

"I got a frantic message from Mikey three days ago telling me that you were coming here."

Oh yeah, Mikey and my family. Of course they'd be looking for me. "What about my texts to you?" I wondered out loud.

"I got one, but then my family took my cell away before I could respond. I've had to use the housekeeper's really ancient laptop, so all I can do is video-chat and check emails. I'm surprised it even has a wireless modem, it's so old."

"Oh, so that explains the lack of responses. And I stopped logging into everything when I landed because I didn't want anyone to track me here. I only sent you a couple of texts from the airport, and then I stopped."

"That was smart, Maddie, because you're in huge trouble," Sayara informed me rather matter-of-factly.

"Yeah, really, so why?" I assumed she was talking about the FP, who by now felt like a nuisance rather than a fearful monster.

"Well, actually, your family is very worried. They know that you came to the kingdom—they figured that out with the passport tracking—but they have no idea where you are and who you're with. Mikey said that they were getting official emergency help and should be here in a day or two. They're worried that you might have been kidnapped."

"Kidnapped! That's crazy. But so technically, Alisha's family could be in trouble?" I asked, now getting concerned.

"Uh, yeah, who's Alisha?" Sayara asked. With that question, I told Sayara everything that had happened since I left home: the plane, baby Sofia, the FP, and my difficulty getting into the country before Matin stepped in.

"Maddie, what in the world were you thinking? Seriously, you just decided to come here? Didn't you know that you needed someone, a guy, to greet you?"

"I know it's crazy. It's totally my fault. I should have checked online. But I had no idea that there were places like this still left in the world. I've traveled by myself so often going to camp or to visit my aunt in England that it's not a big deal to me. And it never dawned on me that there was still a place in modern times where I couldn't do anything without a guy. I know I should have connected the dots, especially when you told me Themi got arrested for just driving. But I didn't realize that it also meant you had really strict laws about what to wear or that I had to have a guy to meet me. And, besides, I texted you and I figured you knew I was on the plane."

"Yeah, I get it. Sometimes when I come back from another country, I feel like I am stepping back into the Middle Ages like we covered in history class. Plus, I guess you didn't know that my phone had been taken away. It was like a whole series of comical mishaps. It would be funny if it wasn't our real life! You're just so lucky you're safe, and I'm grateful because I would have felt so guilty if anything had happened to you. You came all this way thinking you could help me and Themi, and you can't."

"Don't say that, Sayara. You should never feel guilty. You would do the same."

"Maddie, I don't know. I don't know if I would have had your courage to go this far to help somebody. You're really one of a kind."

"Thanks, but I think you would. We have go to the distance for each other, otherwise, how can we change things?"

"Maybe, Maddie. I'm sorry I didn't tell you more about all our weird rules, like needing a man to escort you. We never got to talk about that in the Bahamas, but I hate it, too. So does Themi."

"Yeah, everyone seems to, including Grandma Danah and Grandpa Mansur. You'd love them." Going on with the story, I filled Sayara in on all the details of the past forty-eight hours since I'd been in the kingdom.

"I'm so glad that Alisha found you. There are some really wonderful people in my kingdom."

Her words were telling: *my kingdom.*

"Hey, Sayara, what gives—you never told me you were a princess! Really? Do you have a crown? Do people bow in front of you? Why didn't you say something?" I had a million more questions.

Sayara laughed into the phone. "Oh, Maddie, you're always so ridiculous. Yeah, it's true, I was born a princess, but I don't feel like one. My family isn't powerful like the other main royals, or even Themi's family." Grandpa Mansur had told me earlier about the core group of powerful royals. It was making more sense now. She went on, "Please don't tell Mikey."

"Mikey?" Puzzled, I added, "Okay, why not? What's the big deal?"

"Well …" Sayara paused with a slight playfulness in her voice. "Well, you know, um, so, um, Mikey and I, like, uh, have been talking a lot online."

"Yeah, and so?" Where exactly was Sayara going with this?

Sayara quickly clarified, "Um, we're really mainly talking about you, that's all. Just trying to find you, that's what we talk about the most, but …" She couldn't stop herself at that point and rambled on. "Um, plus, you know, he's so funny and tells great stories about when you guys were younger and the kids at your school. And, like, he treats me so normal, just like you do. No guys I know treat me that nicely or politely. He sends me these really sweet messages. He asks my opinion about how to find you, and, you know, we've been talking about all sorts of stuff, and, you know, he might get all weird on me if he knew I was a royal. I just want to be treated like a normal girl like you … and, and … you know … he's really sweet and … and cute … oh, Maddie!" Sayara was stammering and rambling. Something had changed.

"No way, Sayara, you have a crush on Mikey!" My Mikey, who'd been like my best buddy since we were in diapers, and Sayara? I should have seen it coming from that first video chat. It was kinda sweet, but it seemed to be too much happening way too fast. "Does he know? No, wait, does he have a crush on you, too?" I remembered he had said she was really pretty that first day he met her online.

"No, no, no, Maddie, you're totally wrong," Sayara insisted. "We're just friends. That's it."

"Uh, hello. I am so not buying that. Rule number one—denial means fact. You have a crush. I think that's so cool, my buddy and my new friend! Wait until Mila finds out."

"No, no, you don't understand, Maddie! I'm not allowed to even talk to a boy, let alone like one." Oh, those kingdom rules again! It seemed my eyes were rolling nonstop these days. Thank goodness no one could see them.

"*No one* can know, Maddie," Sayara pleaded emphatically again. "Please promise me. Not even this new Alisha you met and her family. I am already in so much trouble. I can't bear to hear any more about how I have been a disappointment to my family."

"You can't ever be a disappointment, Sayara—you're too perfect. Who said that to you?"

"My parents, Themi's parents, everyone! Maddie, it's a long story, but when I came back, I tried to defend Themi. Her dad, my uncle, is furious at her for driving and getting arrested. He told her that she has humiliated the family by breaking the rules so publicly and has brought shame to them all. And then the whole jail thing—he had to pull some strings to get her out right away. The other seven women are still in jail. He said that Themi was good-for-nothing and a complete nuisance. I was so mad that I raised my voice, which I am never allowed to do. But I had to tell him that he has no idea how stupid the rules against girls are and that Themi was more courageous than him for standing up on behalf of all girls and women. I was defending Themi, but all my family could hear was that I had been brainwashed by her. They thought I was just parroting her words. They keep calling me a stupid child and saying that Themi has been a bad influence, and that as a girl, I couldn't possibly know what's best for myself. I'm sick of being dismissed as a useless girl!"

"Me too! Well, sorta." Once again, Sayara and I were bonding over our frustration at the outside world. "I am so tired of everyone assuming that just because I'm thirteen, I can't possibly understand issues about rules and laws. But I don't get the whole thing about why it's useless to be a girl." I hadn't really encountered people being mean to me because I was a girl. Only treating me like I was immature, which I was really sick of.

"Here it's different, Maddie. A girl has less value. I don't really know why. It's just the way it is, and everyone just accepts it. Themi tried to change it, but we're now both in jail at home!" It was late and we needed our sleep, but at that moment there was a sympathetic bond between us that I could tell would last a lifetime.

She went on, "My father is furious at me. He said, 'Don't you dare raise your voice to me! Don't you realize the pressures of having a daughter? We must protect you girls. Our family honor is at stake. It is a huge burden for all the men in a family.' He then yelled at my mother, who was trying to defend me and Themi. 'Stop, woman, you are no better than this daughter of ours. Filling her head with hopes of a life she cannot have. Her place is here in our home and then in her husband's home. To be quiet, only seen. And to create no problems. Do not idealize Themi! Do you understand, my daughter? She can only lead our family to dishonor and misery. How can I make you all see?'"

Sayara told me that she had never seen her father so angry. "My mother said it was more from the fear of not knowing if he could protect us. We are birds in a gilded cage, Maddie," Sayara reflected. I could hear tears in her voice. "We may have all the treasures of the world, but we do not have the ones most valuable—freedom, equality, and respect. Those you have in abundance, Maddie. You are very lucky to have been born where you were. We have totally different lives just because I was born in the kingdom." Sayara tearfully whispered into the phone, "We're not so different, Maddie—you and me—so why does my world consider me so much less worthy than your world considers you? Why am I considered a burden, and you get to be a blessing?" Well, it wasn't so much a question, because I had no answer. I had no clue; neither of us did. But we both knew it to be our reality.

We both had tears in our hearts. I didn't know what to say, other than what was in my heart. "I don't know, Sayara, but there's a reason we met two weeks ago, and now you will always be my friend, my soul sister—my soul twin for life."

Sayara said, "And you are mine. We will always have each other."

"Okay," I said, gathering my energy and resolve as I channeled my inner warrior princess. "Time for us to have an action plan. We're not useless little girls. Listen, if I'm old enough to get my period, I am so old enough to think like a woman!" Oops, more information than I normally shared, but this was Sayara.

"Oh! So you've gotten your period, Maddie? I think I will get mine very soon, too. I heard Dad and Mom talking about how I would soon become a 'woman' and would need the protection of a future husband. They want to get me engaged soon, before I get into trouble like Themi."

"Okay, first off, your period's no big deal. I'll tell you whatever you need to know when you get yours," I told her. I was already an expert, and my period hadn't slowed me down or interfered with sports one bit. "But engaged! What are you talking about, Sayara? This is crazy. We're only thirteen. This is something that we definitely shouldn't be thinking about for at least another thirteen years! We haven't even had boyfriends! Well, you have a crush ..." I started to tease, but Sayara's voice told me she was too serious to be distracted.

"Maddie, there is so much about my country and its rules that you couldn't and wouldn't even want to know. Many royal and rich families want to get their daughters properly engaged by sixteen or eighteen so that they don't get into trouble with boys. I never thought it would happen to me, because my parents always seemed so supportive of my dreams to study abroad, but this whole Themi thing has really changed everything. No one here thinks that girls are capable of doing anything or living on their own without a guy.

"Themi's dad is blaming her behavior on this guy she knows—secretly he's her boyfriend—but everyone thinks he's just a childhood family friend from the royal school. Anyhow, my parents think that if I get engaged properly soon, then I can wait to get married until I'm twenty or so, but having a fiancé will guarantee that I stay safe, or so they think, and most importantly it will protect the family honor. A lot of other girls are now waiting until they finish their studies at the university, but my dad is worried about his status in the royal family and how it will look if I sympathize with Themi and her friends. All anyone ever does here is worry about what people will think and say of the family."

"There's a royal school? Seriously, don't you just get to be normal? Actually, Sayara, we should go to the same university. Maybe we can even be roomies!" I was excited by the possibility that we could live together like Angie and her best friend at university. "Don't worry, we'll figure out a way together to make sure you don't get married until you meet the right guy and you're ready."

"Maddie, really? And how will we stop it?" I could hear the utter disbelief in Sayara's voice. She was sadly accepting the conditions that her parents were forcing on her.

"I don't know, but I'm here, aren't I? I may not have figured out all the details, but I'm here and ready to bust you out of home jail! Girls can do more than everyone in this kingdom realizes. Sayara, you believed the same things I did when we were in the Bahamas. Don't let everyone here get you down or make you lose confidence. Don't let their constant criticism and questioning give you a bad case of self-doubt—you *so* don't need that."

"Yeah," Sayara said gently. "I really give you credit, Maddie—you surprised me. I didn't think you could change anything, and yet you're here. Everyone is looking for you and everyone is talking about why you came here for Themi, so you got their attention. The king has ordered that there be no press coverage so that your sneaking into the kingdom doesn't embarrass the royals more."

"Seriously, the king knows I'm here? Cool. Can I meet him? I think that if I can just talk to him, I can make him realize that these are silly laws. He can then change them so you'll all get to drive, wear whatever you want, and everyone will be happy."

"I love how you make the most complicated things sound simple, Maddie. The king won't be bothered with meeting 'silly little girls' as he calls us. He thinks the rules are fine, and besides, he always sides with the FP. But I heard Themi say that his son, one of the more powerful princes, is way younger and may be willing to listen and help. He's supposedly trying to persuade his dad to change stuff. You should come here and meet Themi, and she can tell you more. She knows so much more than me. Even though my dad wanted to keep me away from Themi, the king ordered us both into house arrest together—and I am so grateful that my dad has to listen to the king. I would be going crazy if Themi wasn't with me to keep me company. I have to figure out how to sneak you in." Sayara's voice got softer as she started to think about how to get me into her compound.

"I can climb the wall," I offered helpfully. "I'm used to climbing trees and stuff, remember?"

Sayara laughed. "We have to get you in legitimately, quietly, and for some reason other than me since I am officially not allowed visitors. It has to be legit because if you climb the wall, you could be arrested for trespassing or something worse, and you'd be turned over to the FP. Although I think Mikey and your dad and aunt would be here faster than you could blink if I told them."

"Okay, so now it's my turn to tell you not to say a word, not even to Mikey. If he knows, he might tell my dad."

Sayara laughed. "Okay, I won't say anything, but you're right. He thinks of you as his sister, and he's mad at himself for not coming with you even though you said no."

"Sayara, I'm not some helpless kid. I'm fully capable of taking care of myself, even if I am young and a girl. Mikey and my family should never underestimate me."

"I know I never will," said Sayara. "I'm honored to know you, brave Maddie."

"Okay, cut it out, Sayara. You're so corny. We're not dying or anything. We're just gonna bust you out of your miserable home jail. Do you have a bed and get enough food?"

Sayara laughed sadly. "The opposite. I really am a bird stuck in a golden cage. I have everything I want, I just can't leave or talk to anyone on the outside. So it is really just a jail. But Themi is here, too. We just have to figure out a way to get you into the compound ..." Sayara stopped talking as if she was evaluating the options.

I interrupted, "Just get me into your compound! Then we can figure out a plan."

"Okay," she said. "Tell you what, let's plan on this because I don't know if I'll be able to call you again tomorrow. Come to the compound entrance at four in the afternoon. Everyone is usually still taking their afternoon naps. I will tell Rajiv, our watchman, to let you in. By then I'll have figured out a plan.

Let's have a code word." She paused, trying to think of the perfect thing. "Let's do *waterslides*! Okay? Then he'll know to let you in. And if it's not him at the gate or he can't let you in, then just drive away. Don't try anything crazy. It could be really dangerous for all of us!"

"Got it, and you know, I loved those wicked waterslides," I responded. "We have to promise to go back, Sayara. It's a plan."

Chapter 13

T he next day, just before four o'clock, our black sedan rolled silently up to the gatehouse of Sayara's compound. Our driver Amar cautiously rolled down the window and whispered the code word *waterslides*. Beads of sweat dripped down his forehead. Covert entry was not comfortable for him. Rajiv, Sayara's gatekeeper, nodded his head stealthy in acknowledgment. He waved us in discreetly with the tip of his chin rather than with his hand. His eyes glanced around to make sure that he had not been watched.

Entering the family compound, I was stunned at the grandeur. A long, wide driveway lined with palm trees led to an enormous, palatial home. At the sides of the large palace were four more large homes, two on each side, each with its own driveway. I always knew my family was well-off, but this was over-the-top rich—kingdom rich! And this, Alisha said, was only one of many royal compounds. The king lived in the main royal compound at the official palace. I couldn't even begin to imagine how crazy extravagant it must be.

The driveways for all of the homes were filled with a range of expensive cars—I spied a Bentley, a Lamborghini, a Porsche, a Mercedes-Benz, an Audi, and even a Bugatti at the main home in the center. It's only thanks to Mikey that I actually know what these cars look like and are worth. Every year, he drags me to the big auto show in the city, and he literally bounces from one exotic car to another, boring me half the time with all the mechanical features. But at that moment I was glad I had paid attention. It was mind-boggling that a car could be worth $4 million. I remembered my science teacher telling us just last month that you could vaccinate a million kids for the same amount! Seriously warped.

I couldn't imagine any of Sayara's family riding the commuter train line into the city, or anywhere for that matter. It's something Mikey and I do all the time, usually with Linda, but Dad said we can go in on our own in three years. I took those daily freedoms for granted until I came to the kingdom. Here I wouldn't be able to go anywhere alone, just because I happened to be a girl. Worth less and respected less just because of a twist of nature and my place of birth, no fault of my own.

I finally realized why Sayara kept referring to herself as a bird in a golden cage. Here she was living in the middle of one of the richest places on Earth, and she couldn't do anything she wanted. The FP decided where she could go and what she could wear. Women were never allowed to drive the over-the-top, exotic cars. Why did they have so many expensive cars if the women couldn't drive them? Not for the drivers to drive. I guess because the royal men wanted to drive them. Mikey told me that the most fun of having one of these cars is the thrill of being able to drive it yourself. Apparently that kind of fun only belonged to the rich men of the kingdom.

Rajiv, the watchman, had told us to drive along the road to the back of the main house. We'd see a small, barrack-style gray concrete building in the far back and Meena, Sayara's nanny, would come meet us there. It seemed like Meena and Rajiv really cared about Sayara, just like Linda with me. Grandma Danah had insisted that Alisha come with me. "No going on your own. It's too dangerous," she had said. "You don't speak the language, and worse yet, you're not familiar with our culture and the habits. We can't risk anything happening to you, Maddie. We don't have the kind of power that Themi's royal family does, and we couldn't help you if they chose to harass you or arrest you."

It was a little scary, going into the den of the lion. I knew Sayara was here, but so was the mean uncle, Themi's father. He was one of the royals, a total control freak from what Sayara had told me. The king had put them under house arrest, with Themi's father on guard to watch over them. And if he caught us, he could have us jailed too, and not likely in a nice house like Sayara's, but in the horrid prison that Themi was first sent to!

In the back behind the flower gardens, Amar stopped the car, and Alisha told him to go find Meena. Just as he was about to get out of the car, there was a tapping on the back passenger window. Alisha lowered her window, and a young girl who looked not much older than my sister Angie stuck her head in and asked, "Maddie? Are you Maddie?" It was clear she had been running. Her voice was breathless and her face was uncovered, with sweat beaded gently on the sides of her forehead.

"Yes, I'm Maddie. And this is Alisha."

"Friend?" she whispered.

"Yes, Alisha is my friend. Where is Sayara?"

"Come, I am Meena. Follow me." She motioned for us to follow her, using her hand to tell Amar to stay with the car. She indicated that we should both cover our faces with our veils so that no one would recognize us. We began to walk through a narrow path along the back where there was a row of one-story buildings. This was where the help lived, and these really did look like jails. Made of gray concrete, they were in stark contrast to the beautiful, luxurious main houses. The barracks were hidden behind tall green bushes.

"Sayara is in the house, but her uncle's spies are watching, so for now, you need to come with me," Meena whispered.

Spies? This uncle was a piece of work. Calmly I stated, "You're a different nanny than Sayara had in the Bahamas."

"Yes, we are many who look after the royal family. I was not lucky to go on the holiday. Sayara's father did not approve that I was playing tag and climbing the garden walls with Sayara last month. He felt she should not be running and behaving like a boy. It will be against the law. Plus, I am almost nineteen, so I shouldn't be doing such things like playing. He took my papers away, and I am unable to leave the kingdom unless they decide to send me home."

"That's terrible that you and Sayara aren't allowed to play around." More rules that I didn't understand or agree with. How did anyone get any exercise around here? I asked Meena, "How come he can take your papers away just like that? Do you mean your passport?"

"Yes, my passport. Here in the kingdom, I'm just a domestic servant, so Sayara's father can treat me as he wants. It's not always fair, but I accept that I am not equal to them. I'm not even a local citizen, so I can't do anything about it. My mother needs money, so she sent me here because I am hard-working and the prettiest of all my sisters so I can earn a lot. I miss her and my family, but I feel proud to be able to support them all."

Alisha intervened, her voice filled with compassion. "Meena, that's good that you can help your family, but no one can keep you against your will. And you are equal to them as a human being. Money does not determine your worth."

Dad always said the same thing: "We may have lots of money, but that doesn't define who we are inside. That's your character. So work hard and be good. That decides who we really are." He'd always add wistfully, "In my line of work, Maddie, a lot of people make tons of money, but they're not all very nice; some are, some are not. They forget to share and treat other people with respect. At the end of our lives, we die with only our conscience, so be kind and treat others the way you want them to treat you." A lot of my dad's philosophy came from Grammy, which is why I've heard the same message from Grammy, Gramps, and Aunt AK. But it's one thing to know something in your head and another thing to try to live it. I was encountering so many new things about people and life in a strange and unfamiliar place that I was having a hard time keeping up.

After a thoughtful pause, Alisha added, "Meena, I know people who can help you. You deserve a normal life."

"Thank you, madam," Meena responded, her eyes lowered at her own personal sense of awkwardness of someone knowing the truth about her life. "It's not so bad. I can handle it for the sake of my mom and sisters. Besides, Themi has also promised to help me once she is out of this problem. Do you think that the king will pardon her?"

"That's why we're here," I piped up. "We need to see Sayara and Themi and figure out what we can do to help them and get rid of these unfair rules."

I was too busy smiling behind me at Alisha to see him come around the corner, but Meena almost ran right into the tall, burly boy—or was he old enough to be a man? He had close-cropped hair and wore a scowl. He barked at Meena, "Stupid girl, where are you rushing to? I've been looking for you!" Then he yelled, "Did you give Sayara my extra cake last night?" His right hand rose behind his head, poised and ready to strike Meena, seemingly regardless of her answer.

"Sir, sir, please, no, I do not know what cake." Meena's voice quivered with fear, her eyes fixed on the large, powerful hand held high in the air.

Perhaps it was my loud gasp as I realized that he was going to hit her that made him suddenly turn his head and see Alisha and me.

"Who is this?" he demanded.

Meena's voice shook as she said, "My sisters. They are visiting me. Your mother gave permission yesterday." At that moment, I was never more relieved and grateful for the giant black polyester tent that covered every inch of me, including my face. Until then, I had been grumbling about sweating under the heavy fabric, but suddenly it was my shield and protector, even though I was bubbling with outrage.

He paused for a moment, unsure what to do. Having an audience for his brutality was not part of his plan, and certainly not over something as trivial as a piece of cake. "You're lucky—I will spare you in front of your sisters. But see that it doesn't happen again!" And with that he stormed off, stomping in his expensive brown suede loafers and designer jeans.

When he was finally out of hearing distance, Alisha and I exhaled. "Oh my gosh, who was that creepy guy?" I asked. Lifting our veils, we breathed a sigh of relief.

"That's Themi's older brother, Hazem, who's been helping his dad keep Themi and Sayara locked in their rooms." Meena's eyes filled with defiant tears. "He's a monster. I was only spared this time thanks to you, but he will strike me another time and for nothing in particular, just because he can, like for a stupid missing piece of cake. It's just how he is."

I could see Alisha's eyes tearing behind the edge of her fallen veil. Her shoulders drooped a little as she tried to explain the terrible realities of her homeland. "Not everyone in the kingdom treats people who work in their homes, like Meena, nicely. It's very sad, but here people don't treat everyone fairly, Maddie. In the kingdom, rich people think it's okay to treat poor people like dirt. It's a terrible embarrassment for me," Alisha sadly continued. "My parents have always said that we should treat others like we would want them to treat us, but here in the kingdom there's a hierarchy based on where you were born and your family. And those born elsewhere to poor families are at the bottom of the pile and are treated very badly. It's really wrong, and I'm so sorry for you, Meena. You seem like a nice girl. Let's try to find a way to get you out of here. There are other jobs, other ways you can support your family. No one should ever be allowed to hit anyone, girl or guy, for any reason, especially just because you're not rich or powerful. Like so many rich royals, he is abusing his privileges—and he is nobody." The weight of her words reflected the realities of everything I was encountering about the kingdom and Themi's predicament.

Suddenly, as if determined to lighten the mood, Alisha changed her tone and added with emphasis, "He's a total nobody ... and if he weren't born a royal, he'd be a low-life pond scum!" Her nose wrinkled and she sported a disgusted fake smile. Meena and I quickly responded in kind in hushed, supportive whispers. "Oh, totally, the worst, the ugliest, creepiest pond scum." Name-calling was the only weapon we had at that moment to regain our strength and banish our fears.

"Meena, can you get us to Sayara and Themi?" I asked, determined more than ever to act.

"Right now, Themi's dad is talking to the guards outside their rooms," Meena said. "He is upset that the girls went into the garden yesterday. He is under strict orders from the king, his older cousin, to keep the girls in house arrest, locked in their rooms with no Internet, cell phones, or visitors. Both the king and Themi's father are very controlling and old-fashioned. They don't want any changes to the rules and believe that girls need to be obedient and under the control and the protection of their families," Meena informed me. "But Sayara knows you're here. Rajiv was able to signal us when you arrived. There's a back way into their rooms, but we have to climb in through a window as their patio door has been locked with an extra padlock."

We followed Meena through some tall shrubs, darting in between trees, trying to blend into the pretty gardens despite looking like three bleak, black mounds of soil. Coming close to the side of one of the smaller houses, Meena crept quietly under a large, curved bay window. She tapped gently three times, and the window slowly opened a crack. A face peered through the glass. Sayara! At long last! I was so happy to see her face, I almost blurted out her name, but Alisha's hand quickly covered my mouth.

"Hush, Maddie," she whispered urgently. "Don't say a word until we're inside, and even then only whisper. We're not safe here!" Meena's eyes blinked frantically in agreement. We were definitely in enemy territory.

Meena motioned for me to climb up into the window. Normally, I am an ace at scaling anything, but my oversized black tent kept wrapping around my ankles and limiting my mobility. Awkwardly I tripped and fell into the room headfirst.

"Oh! Maddie, are you okay?" Sayara whispered in surprise as she pulled back my body tent, which by this point, along with my bright red hair, was wrapped inelegantly in my mouth.

But I was too happy to care. "Sayara! I am so glad to see you. You won't believe everything that's happened!"

"To who?" Sayara asked. "To you or to me or to both of us? What a crazy week. I'm so glad you're here, but you are truly insane—I cannot believe you came to the kingdom alone … and now here?" We hugged as if we were long-lost sisters, and in a way we were.

By this point, Meena and Alisha had climbed through the window more gracefully than I had and were straightening themselves. "Sayara, this is Alisha. She's the person who saved me at the airport," I said.

Our brief introductions were interrupted as a firm, serious voice boomed loudly from the other room. "I cannot believe these idiots! Once again, they're completely going against the spirit of the law!" A young woman wearing jeans and a T-shirt stormed into the room. She had thick black glasses covering very pretty brown eyes, and her black hair was scrunched into a scruffy ponytail. "Can you believe this? Seriously, can you?" she quizzed Sayara as she stuck a newspaper under her nose. Only then did the girl notice us. "Who's this? Oh, it's you, Maddie. Sayara told me about your red hair," she said knowingly, answering her own question with rapid-fire words. "Awesome, you rock—you came all this way to support our movement. Sit down and I'll tell you what we need to do."

Movement? What movement? And Sayara had been talking about my red hair? Can I ever escape my hair? But at that moment, hair wasn't the most pressing topic of concern.

Sayara politely offered introductions. "Maddie and Alisha, please meet my cousin Themi."

"Pleased to meet you. No time for formalities. We've already lost decades, so let's get to work. Did you bring your phone? I need your phone." More speedy demands. I quickly realized that Themi was no gentle, timid creature. She spoke in terse sentences and gave polite but definitely no-nonsense orders.

"Uh, no, sorry, no phone. I didn't realize you needed one. Don't you have one? Plus I'm not using mine so I can't be tracked," I responded in a rather shaky voice. Themi was not what I had expected. I thought she'd be all polite and dainty like Sayara. Instead she was fiery and feisty. No wonder she was protesting the FP's ridiculous driving ban. She seemed very courageous and ready to fight for her rights! For the first time, I wasn't so sure she actually needed my help.

"Wise for you, but no good for me. I need a phone," she said as she reflected matter-of-factly on my decision to go silent and under the radar. But she was relentless in her focus. "You, Alisha—do you have a phone?" Themi demanded.

"Yes," Alisha answered quickly, "but Themi, while it's nice to meet you, I don't think you should use my phone. It might endanger my family, and I need to be careful."

"Why would it endanger your family?" I asked. "And what movement? Sayara didn't say anything about that. Just that you were in jail for driving." There was definitely more to this story than I had realized.

"I need to send out messages," Themi explained. "Alisha knows, and everyone knows, that my uncle is a controlling and mean king." Her voice conveyed both disappointment and dis-gust. "Sadly, he uses his power to hurt the people who try to create change or do good. He may be my blood relative, but it's terrible. I'm ashamed of his lack of human compassion." Pausing just long enough to take a deep breath, she continued passionately, "And, yeah, Sayara was right, I was jailed for driving. Can you imagine that? But it's more than just that. Driving is just a symbol of all the stupid, unfair rules that we're fighting against. Not just the gals, but the guys, too. Do you know that the FP can arrest you if you're a guy and your hair is too long?" She bent down and peered into my surprised eyes and face to gauge my reaction.

"Really?" The more I heard about the FP, the more they seemed like the nastiest school-yard bullies I had ever heard of. And now they were the dress police, too. It sounded even more like middle school.

Themi smiled, satisfied that I was a supporter of her cause. Pointing to my clothes, she noted, "Yep, the faith police are also the dress police, the hair police, and the thought police. If wearing these ridiculous tents with veils that cover your face is so great, why aren't guys forced to wear them? Why do they get to wear jeans outside of the house and never have to veil their faces? I'll tell you why—because the FP GUYS make all the rules." She definitely overemphasized the word *guys*. "They decide who gets to drive, what music or movies are appropriate, and even what we're allowed to think! Totally creepy like a bad sci-fi flick, only for Sayara and me and everyone else living in the kingdom, it's real. It's our daily life!"

Climbing onto the coffee table, Themi continued her mesmerizing monologue. "The FP are now even giving guys a really hard time. Can you believe that just last month, one of our people, Raef, was sentenced to a thousand lashes just because he criticized the FP in a blog for trying to enforce another of its senseless, outdated rules? It was outrageous! A thousand lashes for voicing an opinion!" Themi stood high on the coffee table, her arms stretched out above her head, addressing us as if we were a supportive crowd and she was giving a serious political speech. "We can only survive if we analyze ourselves, criticize ourselves. Faith is also an opinion, but just one opinion. We need many opinions and of all types. But to punish a person so cruelly for having an opinion that happens to be different from that of the FP or the king? Terrible. Unjust. No more, my fellow citizens." She was completely in activist character, awe-inspiring, and practicing for something, which at the time I didn't fully realize was a career in government and politics.

"That's totally nuts," I said in shock, still sitting, sprawled on the floor. "Where I come from, everyone gets to say their opinion. You don't have to agree, but as Aunt AK tells me, we all have to learn to respectfully disagree." It's funny how at the time when you hear these kernels of wisdom, they make no sense, and then days or years later, something clicks and you realize why they're so important. I was used to having Aunt AK around sharing her experiences and opinions. Feeling a little vulnerable and overwhelmed, I wished very much that she was with us at that moment, sharing all that plus a protective hug, something I really needed.

"Yep, your world." Themi pointed her finger at me. "Your world, Maddie, is more fair and rational. The kingdom is not. And that," Themi added with determined emphasis, "that's what I'm trying to change in the kingdom." Her arms opened wide, as if the room represented the whole country. She was rehearsing the role she wanted to play in life. Themi exclaimed, "Make it fair so that all people are treated equally. Rich or poor, men or women. We're all just human beings, right?" She didn't wait for me to answer. "Right. We are all equal. The king and the FP control the courts here, and they can basically do whatever they want. If they don't like what you say, lashes. A woman tries to drive, jail. What's next, that they punish you because they don't like the color of your shirt? Seriously, it's crazy whack. A person can have an opinion. But they shouldn't impose their opinion on everyone else, especially if that opinion decides that half our population is second-class. Women deserve better. We're capable of making decisions and taking care of ourselves in every way."

"Wow, it's really crazier than I thought. So what do we do?" I asked, not sure anymore that there was really anything we could do.

Themi continued. "There's so much to change, it's hard to know where to start. I just … I just hate being cooped up like this, cut off. It's a form of torture. Feeling helpless." Her shoulders slouched as she stepped down from the coffee table. "My friends are in jail because they are not my father's daughters, and that's not fair. You shouldn't have to have a powerful, rich family to be treated favorably, especially as a woman. So I need to help them."

"How can you help them?" Alisha asked.

Themi paused for a moment, her eyes distant as she became lost in a different thought. "I often wonder what my life would have been if I had been born somewhere else, anywhere else, like where you live, Maddie."

"I don't know—I guess freer than here." I had never really pondered my life in that way. What if I had been born here in the kingdom? Would my life have all these limitations? Would I be forced to wear a tent all the time and forbidden from playing soccer or basketball?

"I'm the only one who has truly lived both," added Alisha, "and I can tell you that living with the ability to make choices about all aspects of your life is much better."

None of us could dispute that; there wasn't anything to debate. The only question lingering in the room was *why?* Why couldn't Sayara, Themi, and all the other women in the kingdom have the same freedoms as me and Alisha?

Themi sensed the weight of our mood and the overwhelming sense of frustration at our inability to easily change their situation. Her body straightened a little as she regained her resolve and announced, "Hariz is coming shortly, and he'll bring a phone. I need to make the world aware of our movement and our efforts. That's what we need to do to keep everyone's focus and attention on our cruel rules. I hope the rules will change before it's too late for my generation, another lost one."

My mind missed the movement talk and focused on the name Hariz. "You're gonna have a boy in here?" I was surprised given all the rules. "Aren't there rules that forbid boys and girls from being in the same room?" I looked at Sayara to make sure I had heard her correctly when she had told me that a week ago. She nodded.

"Rules? Smules! I'm sick of rules!" Themi exclaimed as she started to pace again, her hands waving angrily in the air.

I had set her off again. "The rules are made by the stupid FP, who are cruel to regular people. And they're all men. Who said it's okay for guys to make rules for the girls? I will never obey those rules." Her raspy voice paused as if she was reflecting on all the world's problems. "That's what's wrong with all of us in the kingdom—we're just obedient sheep following dumb laws, pretending there's some reasonable basis for them. No one questions anything. Nope. Just dumb laws designed to make sure we royals and the FP stay completely in power and keep all the wealth." She paused again as she reflected on her frustrations. "And, hello! I am a royal—one of the insiders—and I'm telling you that there is something wrong with this system. Money is great; we need it and I love to travel and live comfortably. But with money and power come a responsibility to take care of others and be fair. We royals are letting down our people. I'm trying to get everyone to wake up."

Themi continued pacing anxiously, urgently snapping her fingers at each of us and at no one in particular. Her voice was breathless as she barely took in oxygen. "But people are acting like brain-dead zombies from a really bad horror flick."

She was mesmerizing, a force to be reckoned with. I was on her team for sure. What'd she call it? A movement. A movement to what, I didn't fully understand, but I was on board. Equality for everyone. I'd vote for Themi and her movement any day of the week!

Themi went on, "To be treated differently and badly just because we're girls. The FP fools people by saying that the tents and the driving ban are to protect women, as if we're all dainty and frail." Her arms up and her body in boxing position, she air-punched away the doubts. "Oh, please! It's just a way to keep us girls from living normal, equal lives, and it just makes me feel invisible. The FP wants to hide us. The FP should be more focused on making sure the boys behave rather than stupidly trying to pretend that they're protecting girls by hiding us under tents and in the back rooms. Smart leaders should want all of us to be our best and make the kingdom strong and successful instead of letting only half the population be useful. Look at the other places around the world where women are treated more equally. People are happier, healthier, and richer."

"It's terrible here, that's for sure," I said, "but how would equality make people healthier?"

"Because," Themi exclaimed, "without limits on what you wear and what's acceptable behavior for a girl, you could grow up playing sports and running around. Like you do at home, Maddie."

"Uh, yeah, that's true. I hadn't realized that. Aunt AK always tells me that healthy habits start early in life, which is why she loves to run. My mom plays tennis and does all this yoga meditation stuff. Even my dad does Ironman competitions, where he has to run, bike, and swim really intensely!"

"Exactly," Themi said. "You play soccer, your aunt runs, even your mom does a bunch of tennis and yoga. It's because you can wear whatever you want outside of the house, and no one tells you what a girl is *allowed* to do." She emphasized the word *allowed* for my benefit. "Can you imagine trying to run a marathon in this tent?" She pointed to the heavy black material swallowing my body. Mimicking wearing one herself, she lamely tried to twirl in a circle before falling down. I thought of Mila trying to dance ballet in a tent. She'd probably trip all over the place.

"It's true, Maddie," Sayara's voice chimed in. "Remember I told you my mom was so mad that Rajiv was teaching me how to play soccer? She forbids it. Says nice girls don't play rough."

"What a miserable situation!" My thoughts came tumbling out. "My mom tried to tell me lame stuff like that too, but my dad loves that I play on the coed soccer team. I would really hate it if someone told me that I couldn't do anything just because I'm a girl. Seriously, that would stink!"

"Totally stink! Can you imagine back in your home if you had to follow different rules just because of the color of your skin or hair? Or what if you had to wear a big *G* for *girl* on your shirt to mark that you're different? People couldn't play soccer with you—they couldn't slide tackle into you because they wouldn't be able to touch you! We need to give the FP a permanent red card and eject 'em from the game," Themi continued. "I can't figure out why people put up with unfair rules and attitudes against girls. Why is it okay for *any* faith to discriminate against girls? Why do we tolerate discrimination of girls but not of anyone else? Seriously, what gives?"

I had only a moment to absorb the intensity of her words before a gentle tapping came at the door. A figure cloaked in a black tent entered, pushing a cart with trays of food. There were cakes—I always see the desserts first—cheeses, meat pies, fruit, and dishes I didn't completely recognize. This home prison was really luxurious! Sayara had told me that she and Themi were in a mini suite within one of the side houses. They each had a huge bedroom and their own bathroom, and they shared a common sitting area. Meena or one of the staff often delivered carts of food. All the staff were on the side of the girls, and showering them with their favorite food was the only safe way to show their support.

Bending over the cart, inspecting each dish, I was engrossed evaluating the food options when the quiet, tall figure pushing the cart flipped off the black tent, revealing ... he was a guy!

"Hariz, excellent," Themi declared, looking satisfied. "You have come with phone and food, two essentials. Well timed."

"I aim to deliver and please," the handsome young man said with a gallant tip of his head, a friendly wink, and a mischievous smile. His face was kind. Looking at Alisha and me, he asked, "And you are?"

"This is Maddie and Alisha," Sayara informed him. "Maddie is my friend I met in the Bahamas, and Alisha has been helping her here in the kingdom." And with that beginning, Sayara and I filled Hariz in on the rest of my adventure and how Alisha and I got into the compound.

Hariz was surprised. "I am in awe, Maddie, that you've been so resourceful at not getting caught. It's not easy, and I often have to sneak around our FP myself. Actually, most young people get used to sneaking around the FP just to try and live normal lives. The FP is a huge nightmare and a pain in the you-know-where. They make all of our lives miserable. My buddy, Bodhi, is now the deputy prince for his dad, the king, so he's trying to free the kingdom from the evil clutches of the FP, but he tells me it's not easy."

"Whoa, time out," I called. "You know the king's son?"

"Uh, yeah, we went to school together at the princes' royal school. Well, actually, it's a school for the royals and some of the really rich, connected kingdom families like mine." Hariz took a deep, cynical bow at his own words. "Bodhi's two years older, but we played on the same soccer team. I was a seriously better goalie, but don't tell him. He thinks he's better in everything," said Hariz with a smug smile.

"You have to get me to see the king!" I demanded.

"No can do. The king won't meet with a girl," Hariz said. "Besides, Themi is his niece, and he's furious with her protest and tweets. Being plastered all over social media makes him look really bad. Like an old-fashioned, tin-pot dictator."

Themi nodded in acknowledgment but protested, "Well, he is totally acting like a dictator. Listen, I'm only doing what's right, and we're only family by blood. It's not like the king knows anything about me or any of the girls in the kingdom. He doesn't really care as long as he can stay fat, rich, and safe. We may be family, but I completely disagree with him."

I thought for a moment. "Maybe I could talk to his son, then—what's his name?"

"Bodhi," Hariz replied. "That's actually his nickname. His real name starts with Najdah and a bunch of really long, formal old family names; I don't even remember them all. But he's really cool and not at all uptight. He thinks like us, but he doesn't have any real power yet. I don't know that he can make any changes, but I guess we could try talking to him. Didn't think he had much sway with his dad on these issues. He's kind of intimidated by his dad."

"Well," I said impatiently, "it's time to think about it! We have to find out and try every option. Let's go talk to him and see if he can get us in to see his dad. Maybe we can persuade him if we talk to him directly." My hand on the doorknob, I was ready to walk out the door to see Bodhi. Advance planning was not one of those things that I spent much energy on. I was a girl of action.

"Uh, hello people," Sayara chimed in. "Am I the only one who is remembering that Maddie can't technically meet Bodhi in person? She's a girl and not a relative. How are we gonna get her past the guards and his advisors?" She turned to me and added, "He's always surrounded by his advisors and body-guards. You can't get close to him. Not even regular guys can get near him, let alone a *girl.*" She rolled her eyes.

Hariz piped up sarcastically, "Yeah, that's right. You're a girl, aren't you? Big problem." His face feigned surprise.

Three days in the kingdom and I was sick and tired of being told that being a girl posed problems. It was so different from home. None of my friends would ever believe how tough the rules were here in the kingdom. But I never met a problem I didn't try to solve. "Okay, guys, if I can figure out how to sneak into the kingdom, you can figure out a way to sneak me in to see Bodhi."

Themi smiled at me. "I like you, Maddie. You don't take no for an answer, do you? She's right, we have to get her in to see Bodhi. It will be more meaningful if one of us girls actually goes to see him. Maddie, you have to represent us. C'mon, let's think of something to get you in."

Suddenly Hariz snapped his fingers. "I got it! I'll take her in, and she can pretend to be a guy. We'll dress her like a guy in a white robe. No one will know if we cover her hair with the headdress. Maybe we can cut it to be safe?"

"My mom will be suspicious if Maddie cuts her hair so suddenly," warned Alisha, "and I'm not so sure that Maddie should go with you alone, Hariz. She doesn't understand our rules like I do, and I can handle an emergency better. I'll come, too. We'll both pretend to be guys and with the men's white robe and headdress, no one will know for sure."

I didn't want to put Alisha and her family in any more danger, but I was so grateful to her. All I could manage to say was "thank you," but I knew she could see my emotions in my eyes. Alisha hugged me and said, "You won't ever be alone. We're family now, Maddie. You're part of my global sisterhood, just as Sayara and Themi are—and we always have our sisters' backs." She winked in solidarity.

"Hey, what about me?" Hariz asked, pretending to be hurt. "Am I chopped liver? Don't I count? I support everything you're doing."

"Of course you do, Hariz," Alisha hastily added. "I guess we should make the sisterhood more inclusive, something else … humanhood?"

"Oh, please!" Themi raised her hands as if to say *stop.* "That sounds really, really lame and corny—and just dumb."

"I agree," Sayara said, eyes rolling.

"Okay, whatever," said Alisha. "Let's just call it the global family or something like that and you're part of it, Hariz, and so are all the guys who support getting rid of stupid, unfair FP rules, especially the ones against girls. We can figure out a better word once we actually achieve what we're trying to do!"

"Okay, that works," Hariz said, satisfied that he was now properly included.

Global family. It was just as Aunt AK always said—your family of birth is one family, and your family of choice includes all the people who love you "as is" and help you out, regardless of whether or not they are blood relatives. This room was filled with people who were now part of my global family of choice.

Themi thought for a moment and added, "I should really come with you, too. In five years, I'll be old enough to run for the kingdom's council. Then one day my job will be changing the laws, not just protesting them."

"Me too!" cried Sayara.

But Hariz was quick to burst our naïve, supportive bubble. "You can't, Themi. The king already warned your father that if you so much as breathe in the wrong direction, he will enforce the lashes on you. I couldn't bear it if you had to endure even one lash." The look in his eyes and the softness of his voice betrayed the emotions he had been trying to hide. It was suddenly clear to all of us that Hariz was in love with Themi. He reached for her hand, and she placed it in his. "And besides, with your sister and brother keeping close watch, you're in great danger," he added, gently stroking the side of her cheek.

Sayara turned to me and explained, "Themi's sister, Nikki, is as strict as Hazem, their older brother, who you already had the misfortune of running into, literally!"

Themi, still holding Hariz's hand, turned to look out the window, half listening and half lost in her own thoughts. She said, "I remember when I was little, about ten, wishing I could have some of the same freedoms as Hazem. It made me really mad that my brother, just two years older than me, could dash out the door any time he wished, ride a bike, play soccer, and swim freely, but I, as a girl, was banned from doing all those things. I still remember wanting to peel off my clothes like my brother and jump in the sea! My sister Nikki didn't really care. She just blames me for not being a good, obedient daughter."

Sayara quickly and gently assured her, "Themi, you're a great daughter and cousin and sister. You can't let Nikki bring you down." Turning to me, Sayara added, "You have to understand that Nikki barely made it through high school. No university for her! She has a 'degree' in shopping and spending the royal money. She's not interested in learning about new ideas. It's just easier for her to believe whatever her father tells her. She wants to please her dad by being the perfect obedient daughter. Can you believe that she actually agrees with some of the FP's rules? It's crazy!" Sayara was disgusted.

Themi interrupted. "Yeah, I know. Last month, she got mad at me for trying to go out without wearing the black tent. I told her if she wants to wear one, that's fine, that's her choice. My choice is not to wear one, and she should accept that, too. She called me a traitor to the family and went and snitched to my dad. She accepts that we should have to wear tents whenever we're not at home, and she doesn't want to drive. She likes having a driver and being able to shop all day, so she thinks it's okay to have the rules against women. She doesn't care about choices, because my dad tells her that he makes the choices for her because he's protecting her." Themi stuck a finger in her mouth to imitate a gag. The demonstration was funny and sad all at the same time.

Sayara added with fake shock, "And worse, she thinks that Themi and I have now brought shame to the family. Nikki only cares about what other people will think of the family and if it will ruin her chances of getting a really rich husband. It's, like, so ancient to think like that, but Nikki can't think for herself and she'd never question any of the guys in the family. She thinks we should just obey our fathers, the stupid rules, and the king. She loves to kiss up, so she would totally tell on Themi if she left this room. Plus, I think that Nikki is a little jealous of Themi and her book smarts. She hates when Themi out-debates her, so she's eager to do anything to make Themi look bad to their dad. Nikki can be a wicked sister if she thinks it will help her look better in front of the family."

"I get that sometimes being sisters is hard." I knew that from my own experiences with Angie. "But I can't believe that Nikki would turn against Themi in public."

"That, Maddie, is another sad reality of my kingdom," commented Alisha. "Women can sometimes be as bad as the men in being really strict and intolerant with other women—especially about how they look, or what they wear, or what they do with their lives, like trying to drive! Some of the women actually report to the FP whenever they see a girl wearing something against the rules. Total betrayal. In the kingdom, to women like Nikki, a girl can have only one goal in life—to be an obedient daughter and then an obedient wife. Sounds like Nikki's only real goal is getting a rich husband."

Oh, that would so never work for me. I shuddered at that creepy thought. I wanted to be like Aunt AK, totally fun, self-made, and successful. But I also know that Angie and my mom think a lot like the people of the kingdom. For them, it's all about if Angie will marry well, like my mom. Ick. How odd, born half a world away, yet Sayara and I were more similar to each other than to our own sisters. But at least Angie wouldn't rat on me—or would she?

Chapter 14

The next day, I found out that the white cotton robes, which the boys got to wear, were thankfully so much lighter and cooler than the depressingly black polyester tents that we were used to. Yet another rule that was different for girls and boys. Not only did the boys get the cooler white robe, but they had the total choice to wear it or not wear it. But for today, wearing it allowed me to hide my bright red hair and every girl thing about me.

The last tricky part was putting the black tents over the white robes so that we could sneak out of the house. It was Alisha's idea. She didn't want to worry her parents or Matin, nor have to explain her decision to come with me.

The night before at the family dinner, Grandma Danah had expressed concern about my safe return back home. She reminded me that I didn't have the proper papers and told me that she really wanted me to call my dad and let him know that I was safe and needed to come home. It would be safer for me, she said, if my dad came to get me so the FP didn't harass me on my way out of the kingdom. Girls couldn't travel without a male guardian's permission, and my whole situation was so unusual that Grandma Danah was worried that the FP would stop me as I tried to board a plane, if they even let me get that close. "Your father, mother, your whole family is probably sick with worry. I know I would be if Alisha did something like this." I couldn't tell her that I wasn't yet ready, that we had plans in motion to change the driving ban, so to quit now would be terrible.

I had said that my parents were traveling without a cell connection. It was a lame excuse, we all knew it, but it was the only way I had to persuade her that I couldn't call right then. I'd do it later, after Alisha and I came back from Sayara's again. We'd created an alibi that we were going back to her family compound the next day. That wasn't completely true, and I hated telling half-truths. For someone who always did exactly what I said, all this going around in secret and disguise felt wrong, but I knew that I had to do it for the greater good of helping Sayara and Themi.

Hariz drove us in one of his luxury sports cars, one with a convertible roof, but it had to stay up since Alisha and I were in the car and we didn't want to attract unnecessary attention. All rich families in the kingdom seemed to love their snazzy cars. We spoke about how cool it would be when women could finally drive, wearing whatever they wanted, letting their hair catch the wind—just like the guys.

It wasn't much of a surprise to hear that Hariz's mom was like Grandma Danah, well-educated and happily working. Hariz's mom was a social rights lawyer, working to protect the rights of the minority domestic workers like Meena and poor people, most of whom were from other countries. The king gave all citizens money, free housing, and all sorts of other freebies so no kingdom citizens were ever really poor, although the royals were definitely richer than everyone else! The only real poor were those who were imported to take care of the luxury homes and fancy cars of the royals and other citizens.

"My mom works really long hours and often loses the cases because the law here is so narrow and strict, plus no one cares much about the poor foreign workers," Hariz explained. "But watching her interact with these workers and the poor families has made me realize that they deserve to have someone fight to protect them. I'm really kinda proud that it's my mom who's doing it. The kingdom can be a little over the top."

"You don't say," I murmured, silently counting the sports cars blurring by as we drove along the kingdom's highways past fancy, shiny skyscrapers. The ancient and the modern seemed to collide all day long.

Hariz laughed. "Money's not bad. It can be very useful as long you know what to do with it and help people with it. From watching my mom, who doesn't get paid much but loves her job, it seems so worth it. But in truth, she couldn't be this kind of lawyer if we weren't rich, so I guess in a way she's been responsible with the money her dad gave her. And my mom is amazing in the work she does. My dad left us when I was little, but my mom's family has helped to raise my brother and sister and me so that my mom could devote herself to these clients who no one cares about. She gives them hope and treats them all with dignity. That's the most important thing, isn't it?" This was more a statement than a question. "That's what most people want, to live with dignity. That's all Themi really wants. I totally agree with her, and I want to help." He paused for a moment, and when he continued, his voice was wistful with emotion. "She's wiser than most of the people I know. Themi is always reminding me that it's hard to believe in dignity when your life is full of restrictions and people constantly tell you that you have less value just because you're a girl."

Hariz turned his face slightly in an effort to hide his emotions, but it was too late. We had seen the depth of his love for Themi in his eyes, and it was sweet and touching.

"Are you already engaged?" I asked softly, remembering that Sayara had told me about her family wanting to get her engaged early and married off quickly.

"Unofficially, yes. Themi's family wanted her to be engaged early, just like a lot of the royals. For me, I've loved Themi since we were little, so it was never too early. We'll get married when we both finish grad school in three years. For now, my family is more supportive of Themi than her own family is. My mom is happy that Themi is outspoken and educated and wants to help people. She loves that Themi wants to run for the kingdom's council when she turns twenty-five, the minimum age required. Hopefully, by that time, Themi will be able to make her own speeches and not have to have me or another male relative make them for her."

"Huh? She can run for government office at twenty-five, but she can't make her own speeches? What gives?" I was missing something … again.

"It's that stupid rule again about needing a man, Maddie," Alisha informed me as she sadly stared straight out of the tinted windows.

"It's true," Hariz added. "The king is now allowing women to run, but they can't actually campaign in front of men. Their voices can be heard through a video link, but no guys are allowed to see them. Their family men can speak for them and travel and campaign."

"Letting women run for council is just a token gesture," Alisha said. "Letting women sit inside the council chambers, buried deep within huge black tents with veils, faceless and voiceless, is just a way to pretend that women are included and progress is being made. Yeah, right." Clearly Alisha was not impressed, and neither was I.

I asked, "What happens to women who don't follow the faith? Do they get to choose not to wear the tent? Do they get to speak to guys?"

"Nope, the tent is a rule for all women. That's why Themi is leading the protest. Being forced to wear the tent, not being able to drive, and not being allowed to talk to a guy—these rules really don't have anything to do with faith. It's just a way for the FP to show their power by having a set of rules against girls," replied Hariz.

The rules were exhausting and suffocating—literally—as I sat uncomfortably, hidden within my black tent. I made a mental to-do list of all the things I wanted to talk about with Prince Bodhi. All this stuff was somehow connected, but I just couldn't help feeling like I didn't have enough life experience to connect the dots or to understand why girls were treated so differently around the world, just based on where they were born. Whether you were a boy or a girl made a bigger difference than your skin color or your family or name or whatever. And in places like the kingdom, it was actually part of the law to make it okay to treat girls and women badly. Go figure. It was so different from my country, where the law is the same for everyone. By the time the laws are changed here, it could be too late for Themi and Sayara.

Once again, I thought of Aunt AK and her spirited commentary on how we have to work with the cards we're dealt in life and make the best of it. "When life gives you lemons, make lemonade." That's what Themi, Grandma Danah, and even Hariz's mom were doing in their own way. They weren't accepting the outdated rules and were trying to make the best of all the unfair laws while still making a difference in the lives of others. But it wasn't easy. Sometimes I think you have to make the best lemonade you can while at other times you need to fight back like Themi.

My thoughts were interrupted by the lights from a palatial compound lavish beyond my imagination. The gates were heavy, ornate, and gold-plated. They covered the length of four lanes, two going in and two coming out. This was not just another rich compound—this was the king's royal compound.

By this point, Alisha and I had removed our black tents and hidden them under the front seats. We scrutinized each other to make sure no loose strands of hair would betray our gender. We needed to be convincing as boys in our white robes and head-dresses. Normally Hariz wore jeans and a shirt, but today he wore his white robe so that we'd all look alike.

"I texted Bodhi earlier and told him I was going to bring some buddies to meet him, so that's what you have to act like, okay?"

"Yep, okay, we're your buddies," I responded, and with that I started to giggle.

"No!" Hariz exclaimed. "No laughing—that's a dead give-away that you're a girl. Your face alone makes it pretty clear that you're a girl, so look down a lot and walk behind me."

"I am a girl!" I declared. "Do I have to curtsy or bow, I guess, since I'm a guy?"

"Here's the deal: Bodhi is very low-key and nice, but the advisors and guards around him are uptight and strict. I texted him to see if he could be alone, but it's hard to know. So just do what I do. And no giggling or talking!" Hariz's face was so kind it was hard to take him seriously when he tried to be stern, but for his sake, Alisha and I straightened up and got ready.

The evening watchman knew Hariz, so he was friendly, waving us in and telling Hariz to park in the usual spot behind the prince's house. It really helped that Hariz was a royal insider. I can't imagine how we could have ever met with the prince otherwise.

This royal compound was huge, with the main palace in the middle and smaller palaces along the way on both sides and in the back. It made Sayara's compound look like a bunch of rustic shacks. Unbelievable. Once inside the gates, there was a long main drive with smaller driveways leading to each of the smaller, but still really huge homes. It looked like even the lampposts were made of gold.

In the dusk, I couldn't see all of the homes, but I managed to get a glimpse of a few of the tennis courts, swimming pools, and fountains. Hariz said each of the king's kids had his or her own home, as did some of the other royal family members. It was like a town all to itself—a really rich town. Like at Themi's compound, expensive cars were lined up in front of the houses and by the garages. Hariz mentioned that there was a helicopter pad all the way in the back so that the king could easily get in and out and fly off to his giant yacht, which was almost as long as a football stadium and could sleep a hundred people. The palace itself looked like it had rooms for that many, and as if he read my mind, Hariz said, "The palace has 146 rooms. The royals live lavishly, and they protect their privacy. They don't want regular people to know how much money they have made from the kingdom's oil."

"It's a shame that they haven't used some of that money to build a better society for all of us in the kingdom, not just for themselves," said Alisha. She was not impressed by the money or shiny stuff; she was more curious about people's insides than about their outsides. She added, "You have to wonder if they really think they deserve to live so much more comfortably than the rest of us citizens. Has anyone around here worked even a day?" I could tell that Alisha was indignant at the ridiculous display of wealth. Her family was well-off, but they shared their excess with those less fortunate.

In that brief moment, I realized why the king was reluctant to change things with the FP—he got to live really nicely, as did his whole family. Why mess it up, even if changing the rules was the right thing to do? Dad always says "Most people don't do things against their own self-interest. It's only when your self-interest butts heads with their self-interest that problems begin."

We had some serious head-butting problems here.

Hariz sensed our anxious mood. "Yeah, most of the royals live totally useless lives. But I promise you, the prince is not

129

like that. He's a nice guy, plus he's completely different from the rest of his family. He's really serious about making good changes and making the kingdom fair and nicer for everyone. Give him a chance."

"We have nothing to lose," Alisha said, adding, "but I hope you're right that he's serious about working hard for change. The kingdom is slipping behind the rest of the world quickly. I see it where I live compared to when I come back to visit my parents. It's not about the fancy technology, but about how people think. And we in the kingdom are seriously stuck in the caveman era!" Her eyes rolled yet again. I knew Dad would have a field day with how Alisha rolled her eyes all the time, just like me. But can we help it if we have no time for stupidity or meanness? I know, I know. Dad always wants me to learn patience. Still working on it.

We drove along a side road toward the prince's house, and once again I was dumbfounded by the incredible extravagance. No expense had been spared in making this over-the-top lavish. A long pond filled with flowing fountains lined the middle of a two-sided road-like driveway leading to the king's palace. Palm trees and flower beds filled the perimeter. The sun had already set, with dusk just drifting in, and white lights shone upward into each palm tree. It looked like a really, really nice hotel, but I had to remind myself that this was someone's home. The king's! It was for just one man, one family. Well, not even the family anymore, since each of the kids had a house within this royal compound. I wondered where the domestic help like Meena stayed. I was quite sure it wouldn't be so nice or lavish—probably more like the barracks in Sayara and Themi's compound.

Hariz parked in a corner slot behind the prince's house. "Bodhi gets his own place. Oh, and he has the most amazing media room. Maybe he can show us."

An elderly butler dressed in a crisp white jacket and black pants opened the door. Even though he recognized Hariz, he maintained his very formal manner. This was the house of royalty, and he did not want us to forget it. Manners and protocol were the most important things. We walked quietly into the grand foyer. Alisha lightly tapped me on the shoulder and motioned for me to look out the glass doors in back, which opened onto a huge patio with a ten-foot-high fountain, beyond which lay a huge private swimming pool, probably just for Prince Bodhi.

At that moment a tall, wiry man with a potbelly hanging over his dressy dark gray slacks came down the main spiral stairs. "Hariz, welcome. The prince is expecting you." His voice was polite, but cold and formal in manner.

"Thank you, Mr. Advisor," Hariz responded, gesturing to the presence of Alisha and me. "My friends and I are eager to see the prince." Our heads stayed bowed down, hoping not to raise any concerns.

"Yes, I will let him know you are here. Please wait." His voice was calm and authoritative, and then, he stared penetratingly at me as if to say *who are you?* My headdress completely covered my eyebrows, the top part of my head, and all my hair, but I felt unsafe and exposed. He paused for a moment and then walked out.

After he left, I whispered to Hariz, "I think he's on to me. He looked at me really weirdly."

"Stay cool, Maddie. You'll be okay. Keep looking down. He's just doing his job to advise and watch out for the royals. But remember, he's loyal to the king, not to Bodhi."

I nodded, although I didn't fully trust the situation and feared for my safety.

Mr. Advisor returned and told us to follow him. I could feel his eyes on me, but I kept looking down. We were escorted into a room off the patio. At one end was a pale green sofa facing a gigantic screen mounted on the wall. At the other end of the room were floor-to-ceiling bookshelves filled with books. Oh, how I would have loved to go over and browse the books, but I didn't dare move out of place.

At that instant, a tall, lanky young man dressed in jeans and a blue button-up collared shirt bounced into the room. "Hey, dude, how goes it?" Prince Bodhi and Hariz fist-bumped and hugged.

After Prince Bodhi told Mr. Advisor that he could leave and we were safely alone, Hariz turned and introduced Alisha and me.

"Pretty good, faking being guys. I didn't know until you told me. I can now see tiny wisps of red hair." Prince Bodhi smiled.

I pushed those loose strands back under the headdress. "Why do you call him Mr. Advisor?" I asked, as it seemed odd not to use his name.

"In the kingdom," Bodhi explained, "people are identified by their job or title rather than their individual name. Just how it goes around here. Tell me," he said, turning to Hariz, "what's up? What's with the urgent texts?"

Hariz filled him in on all of the details of my arrival. Prince Bodhi didn't seem surprised by his cousin Themi's family or how badly they had been treating her and Sayara.

Prince Bodhi turned to me to explain, almost apologetically, "We're on the same side, Maddie. I want to change these unfair and very outdated rules of my father's generation, but the FP is incredibly powerful, and if they want, they will just attack me. My father realizes that the FP have too much power, but it's not so easy to change things, as many people falsely believe that the FP are wise and know best."

"No way!" How could anyone trust the FP?

"Yeah way, Maddie. A lot of people have grown up always thinking that the rules are right, and they don't like to question things. Change makes them nervous, so it's easier to believe some old, bearded dude than to actually research, think, and learn for yourself. Plus, not everyone goes to a proper school in the kingdom. I'm trying to get my dad to change that, too. To get rid of the faith schools as main schools. People can go to them on the weekends like extracurricular activities, but not as their main source of education. Otherwise, we're gonna be a kingdom of dummies!" He seemed so nice and sensible, it was hard to imagine that he was one of the main royals. All this change seemed like a lot for even this young prince to try to take on.

"You're right," Hariz spoke up, "it's a tough road, but that's why we have to work together. Bodhi, you have to figure out how to persuade your dad to release Themi and the other women. It was a protest, and they shouldn't be arrested for just a peaceful protest. That's how change will happen, by letting people have the courage to protest peacefully, say what they want, and debate properly."

"Yeah, I know, especially Themi." Prince Bodhi patted Hariz on the shoulder and smiled. "Don't worry, dude, we're gonna get your future wife—my cousin—cleared of this mess. But she's right, you know. I gotta hand it to her, she's got guts. She's not like my sister or my other girl cousins! Some of them are willing to accept all these limits to their freedom just so they can live hassle-free, well-off lives. Even my own mother said to me last week that if she wanted to do anything, she'd just go on holiday to a country where she could drive and wear what she wanted and then come back when she got tired. I told her that's not fair to the other women in our kingdom, but she didn't care. 'Not my problem, honey,'" he mimicked in a high-pitched voice. "And she's my mom!"

She sounded just like my mother whenever I mentioned a troubled spot or people who needed our help. Oceans apart, our mothers could have been twins.

"Hey, dude," Hariz said, "your mom was always like that. She always just followed whatever your dad and her dad before that said. It's hard because she's been taught that from the moment she was born. Going against the rules can be hard for someone like her who needs and wants to be accepted by her family and culture. The pressure to be obedient is really intense. You can't change her, and she doesn't want to think for herself now. Too late. As my mom always says, you can love her, but you can't change her, and you don't have to agree with her. Do what you think is right, but I gotta say, be careful."

"Be careful?" The question shooting through my mind slipped from my lips as well.

"Yeah, Bodhi is a target for the FP and the members in his extended royal family who don't agree with him," Hariz explained.

"Target? In what way?"

"Maddie," Prince Bodhi started to politely explain, "there are a bunch of folks who would rather that I didn't exist. They don't want to change the rules or bring equality to everyone, rich or poor, man or woman. The FP wants total obedience so that they can keep all the power, and my rich extended family wants to keep all the money. The royals are terrified of losing their money and control of the kingdom, so some of them are plotting against me. But I trust my father will protect me."

"Oh, so that explains the extra guards," said Hariz.

"Yeah, there were some death threats that the FP encouraged last week after Themi's protest. The FP is accusing me of supporting her, which I actually do, although I didn't officially say so last week. So the FP is accusing me and my advisors of trying to disobey the faith, but the driving ban has nothing to do with faith, and the FP knows it. They're just worried that if they remove the driving ban, it will open the floodgates. Then what's next—being able to listen to any music that you want? How scandalous! We're fixated on the wrong issues. Meanwhile, everyone our age gets dumber because our schools don't teach us anything useful, and then we have no jobs."

I was still thinking about those death threats. The FP were a nasty lot. I said, "What about that guy Themi mentioned who had some opinions and your dad sentenced him to a thousand lashes?"

"Yeah, that was a bad move by my dad, but he had no choice. The FP made him issue the sentence of lashes. My dad's not a bad guy, but he's afraid of the FP and he doesn't like change or chaos. The royals have had an awkward coexistence with the FP, and both sides usually look the other way. That poor guy got fifty lashes, which was really cruel and painful, but by then, I·was able to persuade my dad not to let anyone in the FP give the guy the remaining 950 lashes. I couldn't say anything publicly, but I was really ashamed on behalf of my dad and our family that such a brutal punishment was done under his name. It was a stupid number anyhow. Anything more than zero is ridiculous. The FP just randomly tosses out big numbers without any rhyme or reason. It makes them feel powerful. They're just bullies with bellies and beards."

It brought back my first encounter with the FP—overgrown guys with dark sunglasses and fat bellies who pretended to be cool but were actually total losers. I couldn't help smiling at that. Hariz's voice brought me back to the conversation.

"It helped," Hariz added, "that many people around the world protested online and a few presidents of other countries talked to your dad privately, too."

"Yeah, that was embarrassing for my dad." Prince Bodhi shook his head. "My family controls all the papers and TV in the kingdom, so they were banned from mentioning it, but my dad didn't realize that the foreign press would pick it up. My dad wants to be seen as a fair guy, so he was really surprised when everyone outside the kingdom was upset with the lashes. He's just clueless. I love him, he's my dad, but I don't always agree with him. I hate that he still listens to the FP and that he harasses journalists. Sometimes I think that if he wasn't my dad, I'd be one of the protesters!"

Prince Bodhi turned to look out at the lush garden and pool. "The truth is my dad doesn't really have any friends. He always tells me how lonely it is at the top. You never know who's out to get you or maybe even kill you. So my dad has never really talked to anyone outside his small group of advisors or cousins and uncles, who know him a little. But they don't really talk about stuff, not like you and I talk, Hariz."

Prince Bodhi looked melancholy. "My dad's never met regular people like you, Alisha, and your family. He's never gone into an ordinary home. He gets caught up in the protocol and benefits of being all royal and whatever. And his advisors are all old geezers who love their power. They don't want things to change, either. And as for women? Seriously, he's never even had a normal conservation with a girl or a woman, not even my mom." Bodhi paused and sighed as he added, "My mom—I love her too, I mean, you know, she's my mom—but I have nothing in common with her. Books, education, and thinking are just not her thing. Neither, really, is being a mom. My nanny totally raised me."

I couldn't help saying, "Mine, too!" I loved Linda and was grateful she was part of our family.

Prince Bodhi said, "Then maybe you know. The good life, money, Louboutin shoes, Chanel suits, Prada handbags, and luxurious spas, that's my mom's thing."

"I know the feeling," I said.

Then, with the sheepish guilt of a son caught criticizing his mother, Prince Bodhi added, "But in fairness to her, when she was young, girls like her were pampered like little pets and expected to just be pretty and obedient so that they would marry well. It's exactly what I hate and would never want for myself. But here women couldn't study beyond high school. Marriage was the only option. At least she was hugely successful, lucky to be chosen by my dad and his family—the marriage jackpot!"

I smiled in the spirit of camaraderie. His mom seemed a lot like mine. Only my mom had options, yet she still chose to live the easy life and did not want to work, in the house or outside of the house. She wasn't accomplished like Grandma Danah, Alisha, Grammy, Aunt AK, or Mikey's mom. And she wasn't an involved, kind, and caring mother like Mila's mom, but it was her choice. Wasn't that key, to have options, to have choices? To me, life isn't one size fits all. I know that I get to decide what works best for me in every part of my life. Shouldn't Sayara and Themi get to have those same choices, too?

I wondered about the girls I was meeting here, what they might do and choose if they had options in all parts of their lives. "Even stupidity and ignorance are choices—not very admirable ones, but choices nonetheless," Aunt AK would always say. "We should all have the right to make choices and then own up to them."

Prince Bodhi continued to vent. Our presence seemed to be a relief for him, a chance for him to finally say everything that was on his mind without worrying who he would anger. "My dad's old. In the old days, they didn't always treat non-royals or women nicely," he confessed. "Well, even where you come from, Maddie, girls or even people of color didn't have a lot of rights just a hundred years ago. A lot has changed, and we need those same changes here, too. My dad hates change and is really strict about rules, but now he is starting to realize that the rules themselves may be faulty. So in the end, my dad agreed to suspend the lashes indefinitely. He wouldn't totally let the guy go. My dad said he has to preserve his own dignity in front of the kingdom's subjects. It wouldn't look good for the king to change his sentence based on public pressure—people might think he's weak. But really I think he was weak in letting the FP sentence the guy in the first place, just for having an opinion. I think my dad is still very afraid of the FP. They have become so powerful like—what's it called in Greek mythology?—that huge monster that keeps growing heads every time you cut one off."

"A Hydra," Alisha said. "It was a nasty monster called the Hydra. Every time its head was cut, it grew two. Yep, a perfect way to describe the resilience of the FP. My dad says that the kingdom was once free and kind of modern in thinking and rules, but your grandfather fed that FP monster starting fifty years ago, and now we're all stuck with an indestructible, power-hungry demon. Now the only things that are modern are the glass buildings and the fancy cars. So sorry, but it's your family's fault and now, for all our sakes, you have to figure out how to fix it."

"Yeah, your dad is right," Prince Bodhi admitted somewhat meekly. "It's not something my dad remembers with pride, but in private he admits his dad, my grandfather, made a huge mistake. That's what I'm trying to change, and I've been fairly unpopular."

"I've heard of the death threats against you, Bodhi dude. You need to watch your back. You never know who's listening and watching and waiting for you to screw up," Hariz warned.

"Yes, I know, but I would be ashamed of myself if I didn't use my role as the prince to create a better life for everyone in the kingdom. I have a responsibility as a royal. And seriously, dude, threatening me with the inevitable is stupid. We all die, we're just negotiating the time and manner."

"Whoa, that's some serious deep thinking ... are you still the same Bodhi who used to take out players with the meanest slide tackle?" Hariz laughed. "You sound like you're a hundred years old."

Prince Bodhi snorted a laugh. "Take a hike," he said to Hariz as his serious mood lightened and he playfully dismissed Hariz's backhanded compliment. "I'm still just a kid—at least that's what my dad and all his advisors keep saying. Just a naïve kid." Prince Bodhi explained with some regal eye rolling, "In the kingdom, we're always just someone's kid until we're like seventy, then we're the elders for a few years before we die. It's really hard to convince the older generation that we should be treated with respect in our twenties and that we're capable of being responsible, too. Like in your country, Maddie. By the time people graduate from university, they're expected to be self-sufficient in every way. Here everyone just stays at home until they get married, always their parents' child. And parents are to blame as well for how they pamper their kids. Like my dad and mom totally spoil my older brother, who should be getting off his back end and working for the kingdom. Instead, he's always finding new reasons to waste his time and the family money. He's always sailing across some sea or racing motorcycles across the desert. That can be fun, but not all year round!"

Prince Bodhi's face and voice showed his growing frustration with his family. "I know, he's my older brother, but he hasn't worked a fair day his whole life, and my dad lets him get away with it because we're royal," he said cynically, his fingers making air quotations around the word *royal*. "He's the one who makes our family and kingdom look lame, every time one of the splashy foreign tabloids has pictures of him partying in some big hotel somewhere, spending obscene amounts of the kingdom's money. He thinks I'm boring, his 'serious' little brother telling everyone how to fix things. But someone has to do the hard work! My brother and his friends can't be bothered to do any real work—they never have and never will!"

Prince Bodhi's feelings toward his older brother seemed just like the feelings Themi and I had about our older sisters. I guess every family, no matter where they live, has the same weird relationships and feelings. We don't get to choose our family. I wondered what life would be like if we could—what would I choose?

I became lost in my thoughts while Prince Bodhi poured us all some fresh lemonade that one of the staff had left behind. He was far more normal and down-to-earth than I'd expected. He offered us some desserts from a tray filled with all sorts of cookies and cakes—my favorites. Seriously, every place I went to in the kingdom, there was always tons of food.

Suddenly the double doors to the room were flung open. "There, arrest them!" a fierce voice barked. Arrest them, them who? Within a second, I was thrown to the ground, facedown. I felt a heavy pressure on my back, like a foot, and I couldn't look up. I was scared out of my mind.

"What is the meaning of this?" Prince Bodhi demanded very loudly. "Have you gone crazy, Mr. Advisor? These are my friends! Release them at once." I could see the tops of his shoes in front of me as he moved the shoe from my back and started to lift me by the shoulders. Once I was standing, he went to Alisha and did the same with her. I could see about ten body-guards with machine guns surrounding us.

"What is the meaning of this?" Prince Bodhi demanded again.

"Your Highness, these two are girls—females! They have illegally entered the palace, and they have threatened you."

"In no way have they threatened me. They came with my friend Hariz, and I have welcomed them."

"Your Highness, it is illegal for these commoner girls to be in your presence. Girls are not allowed to talk to the male royals. Your father has ordered their arrest." Mr. Advisor confidently one-upped him by referencing the king.

"My father?" Prince Bodhi asked. "What does my father have to do with my friends?"

"Your Highness, you are not at university in England anymore, and you cannot just have anyone you want as friends here. You have to maintain your position, and girls are not allowed. Your father has ordered that they be arrested."

"Arrested on what grounds?"

"Trespassing and mixing with men. The girls have entered the palace compound under false pretenses as boys. If the guards had known they were girls, they would have been denied entry. It is against the law, as you know, Your Highness, for boys and girls to interact."

My knees were buckling under me. Me, arrested? For being a girl? Could this place get any crazier? I had never even gotten a detention in school, and now Alisha and I were going to be arrested for what, pretending to be guys and talking to Prince Bodhi, who was Hariz's friend?

"It's my fault," Hariz firmly announced. "I brought them in. It was my idea. We needed to speak to Bodhi."

"Hariz," Mr. Advisor warned, "it is *Prince* Bodhi to you. Do not forget your rank. You are just boys and do not understand the seriousness of this issue." Turning to Prince Bodhi, his voice booming with anger, he said, "Your Highness, your father can protect you by not letting this incident be reported in the papers, but these girls have broken the law. They should have known better than to come here. They must go to jail and face further punishment. I am your father's representative, and I must follow his orders."

Say what? Go to jail? Further punishment? I definitely didn't like the tone and direction of this discussion.

Mr. Advisor turned to both Alisha and me and commanded, "Criminals, your cell phones. Hand over your phones." And when we hesitated, he yelled, "Now!" We jumped at the intensity of his voice, and Alisha quickly handed over her phone, looking at Hariz and Prince Bodhi for help.

"They are not criminals, and you will not address them as such! This is absurd and wrong. Stay here," Prince Bodhi commanded. "I shall go and correct this misunderstanding with my father. Leave the girls be, and let them sit down comfortably." Prince Bodhi's voice was becoming more royal and commanding with each word.

Alisha and I loosened ourselves from the uncomfortably tight grip of the two bodyguards who had been restraining us. Alisha, who hadn't said a word and had barely breathed, took my hand as we sat next to each other on the large burgundy sofa near the patio window. She bent her head and kept her eyes focused on the carpet below. It was a natural submissive posture that she seemed to understand and adopt better than me. Likely something she had grown up with in the kingdom. Now I understood Grandma Danah's and Grandpa Mansur's comments even better: "The FP has contaminated the kind spirit and common decency of regular people and has made it difficult for them to think for themselves."

My eyes, on the other hand, glanced everywhere trying to absorb all that had happened in the past two minutes. Hariz sat in the chair next to us. Our eyes locked as we tried to silently reassure each other. I wanted to tell Alisha how sorry I was for getting her into this mess, but she wouldn't look up and I was too afraid to say a word. But I think she read my mind, for at that instant, her hand squeezed mine and her fingers soothingly stroked the inside of my palm. Here I was feeling guilty about the mess I had gotten her into, and she was comforting me, having moved well past any issues of anger or guilt. She really was like a big sister.

Chapter 15

Once Prince Bodhi left us, I could see that Mr. Advisor was planning to defy his order to let us be comfortable. After making a call on his cell, which I couldn't hear very well, he stood up and announced that Alisha and I were going to be transported to the city jail for women.

Hariz tried to protest, but it was no use.

"Hariz," warned Mr. Advisor in the coldest and sternest voice I had ever heard, "I would strongly suggest that you sit down and be quiet. The king has ordered this, and you would be wise to not interfere with official matters. I obey only the king. You are lucky that I am here to protect you both. Although to me, you … you are disposable," he said with a flip of his hand, adding, "but I know the prince might think otherwise." I was surprised that Mr. Advisor was so dismissive of Hariz. I had assumed that he would have more say as a guy, but apparently he was an outsider and not a royal—better than us inferior girls, but not by much.

"And who will protect Maddie and Alisha?" Hariz asked with desperation and anger in his voice.

"They are just girls and commoners," Mr. Advisor replied dismissively. "They must face the consequences of their actions. Guards, take them away. Get their black tents first. It should be visibly clear that they are just girls." It definitely was worse to be a girl than to be a commoner, since Hariz was not being arrested or sent to jail. The guards were simply detaining him in the prince's home.

"Maddie, Alisha, don't worry! Stay together, and I will come get you," Hariz called out as the guards grabbed our arms.

"Ouch," I exclaimed, but received no response, no apology. Mr. Advisor's mean eyes were focused straight ahead and not on the unnecessary roughness of the guards.

They led us out of the room and to the back of the house, where an unmarked sedan awaited us. Neither Alisha nor I said a word during the drive. We were both stunned and scared at the turn of events. It was another twist I had not anticipated. Yet I had this intuitive belief that this whole misunderstanding would be cleared up. How? I wasn't quite sure.

I was lost in my thoughts and didn't remember passing anything, but it must have been at least a half hour later when I finally realized we were driving through the main city. Mr. Advisor was on his cell phone in the passenger seat. One of the guards was driving, and I realized that another car of guards was behind us. I overheard Mr. Advisor say, "Don't worry, Grand Master, the prince will not think to look for them at Block Z, at least not for a few days. I am personally making sure the paperwork is incomplete so that the trail is even harder."

I hadn't trusted him when I first saw him hours ago, and now I knew why. He was on the side of the FP. He was more loyal to the FP than to the king's family! A traitor! I looked quickly at Alisha to see if she had heard the same thing. Her eyes were wide in shock. I had heard correctly. I raised my eyebrows slightly, glancing at her, as if to say *what do we do?* She shrugged her shoulders. She wasn't sure. But her eyes were wide with fear as well. It was clear that we needed to think fast.

Our opportunity came just a few minutes later. When we were stopped at a red light, I noticed that my passenger door had not been locked, like Alisha's. I tapped her fingers, hidden under the billowy folds of my oversized tent. I gently tipped my head to the left. Alisha realized in an instant that this was our chance.

It was a crowded two-way street, with two lanes on each
side. I could see a farmers' market on the other side of the two
lanes. I opened the door and jumped out. Alisha jumped out
after me and sprang into action. Clearly her marathon training
was paying off as she darted ahead of me, telling me to follow.
We jumped over the foot median, and as we headed into the
market, we could hear the angry yells of the FP behind us commanding people to stop us. I thought we were doomed. Quite
the opposite. People quickly moved aside to let Alisha and me
in, but when I looked back, everyone had resumed their former
positions, making it hard for the FP to follow us. They weren't
to be deterred, and Alisha and I knew we had to run faster.
"Follow me, Maddie, I know this market. If we can get to the
other side, we can escape on a city bus or at least call Matin!"

I tried to follow her, but she was fast, a much better runner
than me. Plus I had no experience running in the ridiculously
oversized tent. I was tripping every three steps. No wonder
the girls in the kingdom never played any sports. Who could
do anything wearing a potato sack? At that point, my thirteen-
year-old self no longer cared about following the rules, and I
pulled up my tent in one fell swoop to my waist. Dressed in
jeans and sneakers, I was now able to run like me! I took off
after Alisha, the adrenaline racing through my spirit faster than
my legs could carry me.

I could hear the FP guards gaining on me, but I was still
short enough that they couldn't see me in the dense crowd.
Suddenly, an old lady grabbed my arm as I ran, pulling me
to her. She motioned for me to hide behind her in her vegetable stall. Pulling up the large tent she was wearing, she waved
me under for protection. Just at that instant, two of the guards
ran past, yelling at the crowd of people to help them capture
"the criminal girls." No one gave me up. It was clear that
many people didn't like the FP. When they had passed, the old

woman lifted her tent so that I could crawl out. I stood to thank her, keeping my head low and out of sight. I was saved for the moment, but still unclear on which way to run and where Alisha had gone. I searched the crowd and wandered carefully onto the main path. I kept my head down as I tried to figure out which direction to go.

But before I could decide, two powerful arms grabbed me hard from behind. "You foolish little girl. Nobody escapes me or my guards." Mr. Advisor. I hadn't thought he would chase us as well. "Your penalty will be even worse for trying to escape." I didn't even want to think about what it might be. I was relieved that he hadn't realized I had been hiding at that old woman's cart. At least she was saved from any punishment.

This time he tied my hands behind my back, and another FP policeman pulled and dragged me with him back to the car. I could see the fear in the public's eyes. Fear *of* him and fear *for* me, for whatever might happen to me, the foolish "criminal girl." By this point, my veil had fallen to the side, exposing my bright red hair. It was clear that I was not from the kingdom, which could mean an even worse fate. I hoped that Alisha had at least escaped, but returning to the FP sedan, I saw that she, too, had been captured again. Her face had a cut on it. "What happened?" I whispered, fearing that someone had hit her.

"I fell. This stupid tent got caught around my ankles, and when I tripped I hit my head on the ground. And before I could get up, one of the guards had his foot on my back. He tied my hands and threatened to tie my feet and carry me if I didn't cooperate and come back to the car obediently."

We were interrupted by Mr. Advisor, who ended his call and sat in the front seat, informing us that the grand master of the FP was very upset that we had been so arrogant as to try to escape from his guards. "He is furious, as it will make other people think that they too can challenge the FP. No one," he bellowed, "no one disobeys the FP and the grand master. You will pay dearly for this."

We hadn't really thought about it before jumping out of the car. Had we, we would have realized that there really is no escaping the FP in the kingdom.

When we arrived at the massive walled complex, the guards spoke to the gatekeeper, who peered suspiciously inside the tinted windows and waved our car into the bleak, gray jail. This was not the king's private jail that I had heard about, the cushy one that the king maintained for naughty princes and spendthrift princesses who neglected to pay their expensive bills or simply annoyed him on occasion. This was the common people's jail—ugly, cold, and scary.

Hustled roughly out of the car and into the building, we were handed over to female guards. Before Mr. Advisor shoved me at the new guards, his hot breath hissed into my ear, "You'll be here for weeks and maybe years for being so disrespectful of the FP and the royal family."

The two female guards, also cloaked from head to toe in heavy black tents, guided Alisha and me down a dimly lit corridor toward two rooms. I was pushed into one room and Alisha into the one across the hall. Before the doors were shut, we managed to exchange one last sympathetic glance. I had no idea what was expected of us, but I had seen a lot of police shows on TV and guessed that this was the shakedown moment where they'd try to break us and make us confess to something, anything.

I looked at the guard. She didn't look much older than Alisha but her face was expressionless. As I sat down, I caught her glancing at my red hair, always the hair ... but when I turned to her, she quickly resumed her statue face.

Moments later, I was surprised to see Mr. Advisor walk in and slam the table with his hand. He demanded information.

"Why did you break the law and enter the royal compound falsely?"

Whoa, time-out. "I didn't break any laws that I know of. Hariz took us to see the prince to see if he could help Themi."

"Themi?" The name brought new urgency to Mr. Advisor's grim face. "Themi, what do you know of Themi?"

Naïvely thinking that this was my opportunity to explain the whole situation, I went on to tell him how I had met Sayara and had come to the kingdom to help Themi.

"So you illegally entered the kingdom to help another criminal woman escape?"

"Wait, wait, wait. That's not what I said," I emphatically responded. "I said that Sayara was worried about her cousin, Themi, being arrested for a very unfair driving ban against women. The law is wrong and I—"

But before I could finish, Mr. Advisor stood tall and roared, "Who are you to decide what laws are unfair in the kingdom? You are nothing but a girl, and not even one from here! How dare you question the king's rule?"

This was definitely not the path I had expected, but I shouldn't have been surprised. "What's wrong with questioning?" I asked. Dumb question, I know, but the words just fell out of my mouth.

"No one has the right to question the king. Only he can decide with the advice of the FP on the rules. The king is the protector of the faith." Contempt dripped through his words.

"Alisha's parents, Grandma Danah and Grandpa Mansur, said that the driving ban is not about faith," I said, hoping to use their age and wisdom to make my argument even stronger.

"They know nothing about the rules or faith. They are just commoners."

"So wait, you have to be a royal or the grand master of the FP to be an expert on the faith? That really seems unfairly biased. Isn't faith about what's in your heart, not what your name or title is?"

"This is about proper faith and serious national affairs, things that you as a little girl would never understand." Usually when people belittled me because of my age, it made me mad, but for some reason, this time with this pathetic old guy, it didn't. I almost felt sorry for him. He was grasping to justify something that was slipping from his hands, and I could see it in his eyes.

"These are the rules," he insisted, his voice more forceful than his physical stature. "And besides, people are happy in the kingdom. There are no complaints. If there were complaints, the king is a fair man—he would listen." I couldn't figure out if he really believed the words coming out of his mouth, or if it was just the official line.

"Uh, that's not actually true," I said. "People protest like Themi, but you just throw them in jail. So everyone is not happy, and the king should be listening to everyone, not just the people who tell him what he wants to hear. The king should meet with Themi—she's his niece, after all! Then he could hear how unfair the driving ban is." I saw my chance to help Themi make her case.

"Second niece, his cousin's daughter—too far removed. She is nobody to the king," Mr. Advisor informed me, as if the distant family link was grounds to dismiss Themi with the toss of his hand.

"So then how can you say that the king is fair, if he is refusing to meet with Themi and even hear why the driving ban is ridiculous? That's not fair." I wasn't giving up so easily. My dad always says I am the most tenacious person he's ever met, a little like a pit bull, and when I put my mind to something, there is no budging me. Yep, just try me, Mr. Advisor. I was feeling more confident with each word, probably because I could sense he knew I was right.

"Only the king can change the rules." His voice rose an octave in exasperation. "Foolish girl. Only the stupid ask questions. You are no one here. Guards, take her to Building D." And with that, he dismissed me. I was slamming into another one of the kingdom's many walls. Mr. Advisor was unable or unwilling to debate the subject of the outdated, unfair rules any further. I quickly realized that as a prisoner, I could only be so tenacious.

I was led down a long corridor across the outdoor open area and taken to Building D, where I was ordered to change into a gray prison uniform. Later I learned that it was deep within the prison, where the FP kept people they hoped would never be found or released.

I soon came to realize that there were a lot of women in jail of all ages, sizes, and shapes, but none of them seemed really bad to me. They actually seemed kinda mellow. After talking to some of them, I realized that many of them were like Themi and had boycotted some rule that they didn't like. Others were maids like Meena who had protested when they had been treated poorly or were beaten badly by their bosses.

I sat quietly on a chair, waiting and hoping that Alisha would be brought here, too. That's when I met Sara, another woman who had tried to drive. Sara was an engineer who was born and raised in the kingdom and now worked on buildings and bridges for a foreign construction company. "No company in the kingdom would hire a woman, so I had little choice but to work for an outside firm. I just want to be able to work and not be made to feel that I'm second-rate just because I happen to have been born a girl. It's not fair. I have worked very hard at the university, and yet I am forbidden from going to a construction site even for the buildings I've helped to design! I can't even drive from building site to building site. It's ridiculous. All anyone sees is a faceless tent. No identity, and certainly no voice and no rights to be a respected professional."

From behind me, another gentle voice piped in. "I dream of the day that I can choose the style and color of my clothing," declared Jana, who was an aspiring fashion designer. "I just want to be able to drive and wear what I choose. The world has forgotten us women. They think just because we have enough food on our table and a roof over our head, everything's fine. But it's not. So many of my friends in university are warned every day that if they don't properly wear the tent and veil, they will be arrested. I just got sick of the FP and their unfair rules! So I stopped wearing my black tent. Didn't last more than half a day before they caught me. It was one of my women professors who tattled on me. Can you believe it, another woman? But sometimes our families and other older women pressure us young women more than the men. But I don't care. I will do it again and again until they get sick of arresting me."

At that moment, Alisha walked into the open area, commenting on the conversation she had overheard. "I know how frustrating it is. I felt the same way. My mom made me realize that for many women in her generation, they were raised in a culture that brainwashed them into believing that the tent and veil protected them in some warped way, like a shield from sin. And it's really hard to shake that level of mind control. That's why we have to fight against the brainwashing. We can be really great and do good work and lead fun lives without needing the stupid rules or false protections of the black tent. It has no powers—in fact, it slowly takes away our real inner power." Alisha winked at me. "Girl power, that is."

We hugged and sat down together on a flimsy, dusty mattress. "Will anyone know how to find us, Alisha?" For the first time I was nervous about being lost in a black hole, not being found by my dad, stuck in a foreign country in an ugly jail.

"Of course. And Hariz and Bodhi are well aware of the FP tricks. Stay strong and stay patient," she counseled, smoothing her faded prison uniform.

I wondered how Alisha could always be so positive and upbeat. Frankly, I was feeling really discouraged and frightened that we might end up staying in jail. I wished that I had texted my dad or spoken to Mikey. Hopefully Sayara, through her connection to Mikey online, would be smarter in letting my dad know what had happened. I looked at Alisha, who had gotten up and was walking about very quietly speaking to each of the girls and women in the cell, one by one. Someone had asked what she did and when the others found out she was a doctor, everyone wanted to ask her about their health problems. I knew that Alisha was as tired and worried as me, but she managed to put the others ahead of her own needs. I had a lot to learn from her. She reminded me a lot of Aunt AK and Grammy at home. I really missed them.

As I surveyed the bleak, gray, open-room cell, I noticed a young girl about my age sitting in the far, grimy corner. She looked scared and tired, and I walked over to talk to her. At first she didn't know what to make of me and my fire-red hair, but when I smiled, she smiled back. Eager to at least be useful, I tried to speak with her. "Hi," I said as pleasantly as possible given our surroundings. "What's your deal? Why are you here?"

"I was arrested for listening to a new rap song," came the fragile response. "My cousin who lives outside the kingdom posted that it was really a great song and so I wanted to hear it. I know that the FP has banned all pop stars and pop music, but I thought just once it might be okay if no one found out. But they did."

Arrested for listening to rap and pop music? She, too, was just thirteen. Tears came to my eyes.

"Don't worry. I have faith that my father will come for me. I know that he may be upset with me, but it will be better than being in this jail. When I am older," she said, her eyes defiant with determination, "I'm going to live with my cousin far away from this kingdom so that I can drive, listen to music, play sports, and go see a movie in a theater like girls and boys everywhere!"

If the FP didn't back off, pretty soon all the young people would leave this prison of a kingdom! I had taken so much of my life for granted. I didn't even see the things I did on a daily basis as freedoms, but just normal life. Learning to drive, saying what I think, listening to whatever music I wanted, making my own choices about what I wanted to wear or listen to or do with my life—this was just normal daily life for me and my friends. I had assumed everyone around the world had the same liberties. It never dawned on me that these freedoms I took for granted could be taken away from me. There was no freedom here for Sayara, not under these circumstances. I wished I could convince Sayara to come and live with my family so she could be free to make any choice she wanted about how to live her life. But I knew it would be hard. She was as attached to her family as I was to mine. Our families weren't perfect, but we loved them.

Just as I was plotting how to help Sayara, the cell door opened and a woman rolled in a cart with rice and some meat pies on it. Certainly not the kind of feast I had been enjoying at Alisha's house, but I was starved. When the women saw the food, they motioned for Alisha and me to serve ourselves first. Even in these bleak surroundings amongst these women, there was a spirit of sharing and kindness. They knew I was not from the kingdom—clearly my red hair stood out—and everyone wanted to take care of us.

As we sat to eat, I turned to Alisha next to me. I was even more curious now than when I first met her. "Alisha, why did you really leave the kingdom? Was it just because you didn't want to wear the tent anymore? Or was there more?"

"In a way, yes," Alisha replied. "I just wanted the freedom to follow my own destiny as a doctor and a person. For me— and also for Matin—and one day for our children. I am so lucky to have a guy in my life who is kind, smart, compassionate, and who also believes in the same life philosophy as me. For us, faith is a deeply personal, internal thing and should not be held hostage by any FP anywhere. They think that they alone have the inside track on deciding what the rules are or how someone should be true to a faith, whichever one it may be. I love the ideas behind the faith I was born into. The spiritual poems are lovely. But I came to realize that in the kingdom, it's not about faith for the FP. They are using faith to keep power in their hands through fear and intimidation."

Despite our surroundings, I felt that Alisha and I were getting closer. There was something about her, maybe because she was older and smarter than I was. She was like a protective big sister.

Hours later, as I was starting to wake up from a restless sleep, I was surprised to hear someone call my name and Alisha's. The quiet guard indicated with her hand that we should follow her, and she led us to a private room. I was a little worried that this would be another place to keep us. I had felt safer in the larger pen with the group of women. With each passing moment, I was regretting not having answered Dad's many, many texts. He didn't even know where to look for me now.

There was a tap at the door, and to our huge surprise, in walked Hariz, followed by a tall, tent-covered woman. She swooped past him once in the room, her tent flowing majestically behind her, and threw off her veil with the quick flip of her hand. Unlike most of the other tents I had seen in the kingdom, this woman's tent was burgundy, made from a much nicer silk chiffon fabric. This woman was different, and I could see that she carried herself with elegance and confidence.

"Maddie! Alisha!" Hariz exclaimed. "We are so happy to have found you!"

"We are even happier," said Alisha. "Can you take us home, please? I really want to see my baby and my family." Her eyes were full of tears. Here in the private room, her true emotions came through. She no longer needed to be brave.

"We're working on it," said the elegant woman. "But things take a little longer in the kingdom. And finding you both—phew! That was hard enough, but don't worry," she said, winking, "we're patient, persistent, and loud-mouthed!" I already liked this woman. She was just my speed!

"I'm sorry, where are my manners?" she continued. "I'm Sabrina, Hariz's mom." She shook my hand and then Alisha's.

She seemed to be everything Hariz had told us about her. She radiated authority, and she also happened to be beautiful and regal like Alisha.

"So, you do realize that there is no reason for us to be in jail?" I asked, determined to get out of this ridiculous situation.

"Of course there is no *real* reason, Maddie. There's rarely a real reason. But welcome to the kingdom, where the FP and their cowardly cronies do whatever they want. They can make up the rules, judge you, and jail you all in one fell swoop with no checks or balances. It's what I have been fighting against, like Themi. Don't worry, we're going to get you out and make sure the FP apologizes—or we're going to make a big stink about it online and in the media! Luckily for all of us, Hariz is just as keen to support our cause, and he was tenacious in tracking you down in this prison." She smiled reassuringly. Her tone and attitude were headstrong and inspiring, just like Themi's.

Now the dots were beginning to connect. Hariz was the boyfriend and son of two of the strongest activists I had ever met, and he was a pretty intense one himself. Instead of being concerned, I was relieved. I knew this woman would go to the mat for Alisha and me. "How did you decide to be a lawyer?" I asked. It didn't seem like an easy job in a place where women had to wear full tents and veils and couldn't even technically speak out in public.

"Why did I become a lawyer?" She repeated my question as she thought of the best way to answer. "It was really the best thing to do. I had grown up hating the rules but didn't think much about change until I had Hariz, and then I realized his generation would grow up with the same limited life. I realized that if I wanted things to change for my son, I would have to be part of the solution and not just sit around waiting for someone else to do it for me. So after I got divorced, I decided that's when I would go back to school, law school. Everyone chooses to fight in different ways. Using the law is the best way. I had read a lot about amazing people like Mahatma Gandhi and Nelson Mandela, who fought to bring equality to their countries. They both led huge protests in South Africa and India, but they were also trained lawyers so they knew what kinds of fair and equal laws could replace the unreasonable ones. They may have been men, but why couldn't a woman in the kingdom do the same?" She smiled. "And why not me? People always think that someone else will make the changes that everyone wants, but no one wants to be the first to protest. They should start protesting, small and big—it doesn't matter. Just taking action is a huge first step." She paused to take a sip of water.

"I also wanted to learn real global law, not just some half-baked version of faith law that is taught in the kingdom." It was just like what Grandpa Mansur had said about distorted information that was now taught in the schools. Sabrina continued, "The FP here is afraid that if people learn properly they will overthrow the FP, which actually, we probably will!" She said this with another smile and a wink. "The FP is against most kinds of studying. So I went to Newtown, where I knew I could learn everything, and properly. Even though Hariz was little, he came with me, and my mother came too, to take care of him. I didn't want to leave him behind and besides, he was such a cute little baby," she cooed, pinching his cheek gently.

"Oh, Mom," groaned Hariz. That, too, seemed universal, the ability of parents to totally embarrass their kids.

Hariz's mom turned to the closed door and banged on it from the inside. "Guards, open up," she demanded loudly. Turning to Alisha and me, she explained, "I've submitted for you both to be turned over to Hariz and me. Well, actually Hariz." Her eyes rolled ever so slightly. "Our FP rules require that you have a male guardian. With that, we can get you both to Alisha's home, where Maddie, your father and aunt are waiting for you."

"Dad and Aunt AK!" I was so relieved. "How? When?" I stammered. I had so many questions, but I finally felt hope that I would be home soon.

"Alisha's mom and dad contacted your dad two days ago," Hariz's mom informed us. "They were deeply concerned about your safety, but they worried that if they told you, you might run away again. Danah wasn't sure if you were running away or really just trying to help. Turns out you were really just trying to help Themi and Sayara."

Sabrina banged on the door again. "Guards! Where have they gone? Coffee break, no doubt."

A few minutes later, the door opened lethargically. "You banged, madam? It's coffee time."

Sabrina smirked. "Why am I not surprised? It's always coffee time. Please, guard, it's well past breakfast time."

So that was why my stomach had been grumbling. I had lost track of time with no windows to see the sun.

"These girls have not eaten, and we are to be heard by the superior FP judge in one hour. He does not like to be kept waiting." She tapped her watch impatiently.

"Really?" I had no idea who or what the superior FP judge was, but it sounded important, at least the way Sabrina said it. But I felt Hariz's foot gently kick my leg. "Quiet!" his eyes demanded.

Sabrina continued to stare down the guard, who responded disbelievingly, "Madam, I have no notice that you have a court appearance. Where is the notice?"

"Goodness, do I have to do everything?" Sabrina reached deep into her briefcase and pulled out an official-looking document stamped with the FP seal at the top. At that same moment, the female warden, who was older and heavyset, barged in.

"What's going on here?" she demanded.

"Why are your people not more efficient?" Sabrina responded in an equally authoritative and demanding voice. "They do not have the papers for our appearance in front of the superior FP judge in one hour. We have no time to waste."

The warden looked at the official document, rubbing her finger over the seal. Her eyes glanced unsurely at Sabrina. Her head shook for a moment, and then she nodded as she noted the date and time of the appearance. "Yes, it appears all is in order. Guard, release the two girl prisoners to their lawyer. Go get their things and bring them here so they can dress properly." With that order, the guard disappeared.

The warden walked right next to Hariz's mom and smiled gently. In a soft whisper, which I could only hear standing directly behind, the warden noted, "Nice trick, madam. But I know that you have no court appearance. The superior judge is in the hospital undergoing surgery. My brother is his doctor." I gasped out loud.

But Sabrina said not one word. I don't think there was any surprise on her face. She had nerves of steel and stared directly at the warden.

After a pause, the warden continued. "Don't worry. I am on your side and the side of these young girls. There are many enemies within the king's circle. I have been warned to keep you here indefinitely or I will lose my job. But some things are more important, and I, too, want the rules to change, especially for my daughters and their friends. There are too many decent people tossed into prison and for no good reason. Our future rests with you and your kind." Raising her hand to wave over all of us, she added, "May kindness, courage, and peace be with you." She stepped slightly back, smoothed her black tent, and smiled silently. Sabrina reached forward to take the warden's hand between her own. "You are a good person, Mother Warden. Thank you."

I was stunned. Even the prison warden was on our side! No one liked the rules, and no one seemed to care for the FP either.

Once dressed in our own clothes and settled again within the folds of the black tents, we made our way through the prison gates and into the luxurious seats of a sedan. I realized I had not slept well and my body longed for a soft bed. No one said much as we drove home to Alisha's house.

Chapter 16

I woke only as we turned the last corner into Alisha's lane. The hour-long nap had refreshed me, and I was excited to see everyone. Driving into the small family compound, Amar, the driver, beeped the horn loudly. The front door flung open, and Dad ran down the steps, Aunt AK following close behind. It was an instant mob scene, with all of us grabbing and hugging and crying. Matin, holding baby Sofia, Grandma Danah, and Grandpa Mansur all descended lovingly on Alisha at the same time. There wasn't a dry eye anywhere.

Dad just kept clinging to me in a bear hug—or was it me who didn't let go of him? I don't remember exactly, only that we clung to each other an extra long time. "Your mom is sorry that she couldn't come. She didn't feel safe," he finally said, pulling back to look at my face.

"Safe?" I exclaimed. "We were the ones in jail, and *she* didn't feel safe?"

My dad stayed calm, his firm hands steadying my shoulders. "It's okay, Mads, let it go. Just forgive people their weaknesses. Your mom loves you, but she is who she is." He was always making excuses for her, but for now he added, "I know you think I'm clueless about how you feel, but I'm not. I just don't always know how to talk about stuff like that. But Maddie, I'm really proud of you, your courage, your big heart, your spunk. Everything. Still, if you ever scare me like that again, I'll … I'll …"

Aunt AK intervened with her loud, quirky laugh. "What your dad is trying to say, sweetie, is that he loves you. I love you, your whole family loves you, and we're just so relieved that you're safe. Although we have no idea what possessed you to take on such a crazy scheme!" Her long, strong arms came around my dad and me, hugging us close. "But we're so grateful that you bumped into Alisha on the flight. What a lucky coincidence!" Now she hugged Alisha and the baby.

"Ah, but there are no coincidences in life," Grandma Danah said. "Just destiny, and now it's our destiny to have lots of good food and some time to relax. Please follow me." Grandma Danah herded everyone into the back parlor room, with its tables of fresh food and big, inviting floor pillows.

We swapped stories of the ongoing adventure. Dad stayed close by me, alternating between hugging me and scolding me. "Maddie, you've done some crazy things in your life, but this stunt really takes the cake. What were you thinking? Coming all alone to a place like this? You scared the life out of us!"

"I know, I know. Everyone keeps asking me."

"I mean, what could you possibly have been thinking to get on a plane and come to a place you knew nothing about?"

"I know, Dad, I realize that I didn't plan it well at all. I just really didn't realize that there were places that had so many laws like this against girls. It really didn't dawn on me. I just figured people may dress differently or eat different food, but I assumed we had the same kinds of laws and similar attitudes toward girls and boys."

Aunt AK intervened. "Of course you would have, honey. How would she have known, Roger? Unless you've spent time living in other places, you wouldn't necessarily realize the differences or what we all have in common. It's a bit of both, you know."

"I really didn't realize that regular girls like me are treated so differently based on where they were born, just because they're girls. I now totally understand it, not just thanks to Sayara and Themi, but also from everyone I've met here."

"You're incredibly headstrong, Maddie," Dad said, "which I know can be a good thing when you grow up, but sometimes you put yourself in dangerous situations when you don't think through every step. I am just so grateful you're safe. But you should have at least Googled this kingdom or asked someone. Seriously, what were you thinking?"

I could tell he wasn't going to let me forget my lapses in judgment so quickly. "I know, Dad. I get it now. I should have planned better, researched, whatever, whatever, but I really was so focused on wanting to help Sayara and Themi, I just couldn't even imagine that places like this still existed in the world. I'm really sorry, but I had to. I had to help."

"You can help," said Aunt AK, "just do it as part of a team and let us know what you're planning. That way you're always safe. Thank goodness Danah used her better judgment, found your dad's number, and called him." Aunt AK and Grandma Danah locked eyes in sympathetic understanding.

"Maddie reminds me of when I was little and also of my Alisha, both spunky and determined. But, Roger," Grandma Danah said to my dad, "your daughter is not only courageous, she achieved her goal. Her arrest was on the kingdom's evening news last night because of the wild chase through the farmers' market. The FP couldn't hide such a scene! Everyone's curious now."

"It wasn't just good, it was great," chuckled Grandpa Mansur, slapping his knee with delight. "The king hates to report on protests like Themi's, but Maddie, you made them. You made a terrific scene. It would be nice if everyone responded to logic and reason, but that isn't always the case. People don't always get it together because they see the light, but more often because they feel the heat." I was struck by this.

Grandpa Mansur went on. "Maddie, you, Alisha, Sayara, and Themi are managing to put some heat on our FP. I, for one, love it! Make 'em rethink their silly rules and start treating people with the kindness and respect that they would like in return. Who doesn't like to be treated nicely or fairly, huh?" Grandpa Mansur was genuinely thrilled with the idea that the FP was being put in an awkward light.

"He's right," Grandma Danah said. "There's been a lot of media attention on all of you girls, but not all of it is good or safe. Some people love what Themi is doing, and some are angry with her for creating chaos. Right now, we're all lucky that you and Alisha are both safe and nothing worse happened to either of you."

"I know, Mom. I'm sorry for worrying you all. I should have known better—I should have known the risks of defying the FP. Not everyone wants change." Alisha was truly remorseful that she had put her parents in peril.

"That's okay. I know that you need to stand up for your rights. Just please be careful. The kingdom can be very dangerous, but your dad and I are very proud of your courage."

"Me too," piped in Matin, carrying baby Sofia, still sleepy from her nap. Sofia gestured for her mother and settled cozily into Alisha's lap.

Matin, who was checking his phone with his free hand, looked up and informed us excitedly, "Hey, wow! This is amazing. Hariz just told me that thanks to all the media attention, the prince was able to convince his dad to meet with Themi. She's going to get to see her uncle, the king! Maddie, you did it!"

"That's fabulous! That's Prince Bodhi." I was excited and in utter disbelief. I knew this was my goal, but over the last few days I hadn't really thought that any progress would be possible. Stuck in jail, all I had hoped for was to go home! And now, Themi would get the chance to convince the king that the laws against girls were outdated and senseless.

Matin added, "Here's another text from Bodhi ... hey! He said we're all invited plus Sayara! Tomorrow at ten o'clock. We're all invited to meet the king!"

"Really?" I was surprised at the turn of events. This was astonishing!

"Yep, Maddie, looks like you're getting your wish after all. The king has agreed to see us all tomorrow at the same time," Matin said with admiration and disbelief. "I can't believe it, but it looks like it's so. You did it—you really rattled some old cronies around here!"

"We," I corrected him. "We all rattled some old cronies. It's taken a team of us, inspired by Themi, but we outsmarted the old FP!" It had been a wild few days in the kingdom, and we were about to talk directly to the king, finally!

Chapter 17

The next morning, we piled into three cars. Hariz had sent one of his family SUVs for Dad, Aunt AK, and me to ride in. Alisha and her family were in their family car. Hariz and his mom were going to pick up Themi and Sayara and meet us there. It took some effort to coordinate everyone. Themi's dad tried to protest that he was her father and should come to meet the king, but Hariz was quick to point out that Bodhi had not invited him, only Themi and Sayara. Themi's dad was not pleased at being upstaged by his daughter, but he stayed back without further fuss.

Driving back into Bodhi's royal compound, I had a fleeting eerie feeling. The last time I entered this place two days ago, I had ended up in a terrible jail. But this time, I felt secure because I was riding with my family and we had been officially invited. In fact, I didn't even have to wear a tent this time. Bodhi had told us to come dressed formally but as we normally do. Alisha had lent me one of her dresses, as I hadn't thought to pack anything but jeans.

This time, we were going directly to the huge main palace where the king lived. Entering the king's opulent palace, I was blinded by the bling. There was gold everywhere—on the chairs, on the doors ... even the tissue holder was made entirely of gold!

When I talked to Sayara on the phone earlier, I found out that initially the king had refused to meet with me, Alisha, Themi, and Sayara because we're just girls and Alisha is a commoner. But once Hariz told him that my dad was here, it was suddenly okay, because Dad's a guy and a successful businessperson. It didn't seem fair yet again that we needed a man to be heard. At least my dad and Hariz were playing on our team, cheering on Themi's protest.

We were ushered into a huge room. At one end, there was a long, gray marble dais. In the middle of it sat a big chair, almost like a throne. I guessed that the king would sit there. There were rows of chairs lined up on either side of an aisle. The king used this room to meet with his people. We were told to sit in chairs, girls on one side and boys on the other. But my dad—gotta love him—just smiled politely at the guards and sat on the girls' side to my right. It completely unnerved the guards, but they were too timid to challenge his determined, protective grin. Aunt AK sat next to him, and on my left was Alisha's family. Themi, Sayara, Hariz, and his mother were in the row in front of us. We were all on the girls' side of the aisle, and none of us wore the mandatory tents in a peaceful protest. We were a visual force of solidarity. I wanted to take a selfie of us all, but Alisha warned me against it. Who knows what other rules we'd end up breaking, even before meeting the king!

Moments later, Bodhi—that is, Prince Bodhi—entered the room. I always forget to use his title, since he seems so normal and down-to-earth. But Prince Bodhi entered looking extremely royal in a nice dress shirt and pants. The king, tall and stately, walked in close behind wearing his traditional white and gold royal robe. We received a signal to stand, which we did, although I could hear Grandpa Mansur cough and whisper, "Respect should be earned." Out of the corner of my eye, I saw Grandma Danah tap Grandpa Mansur's hand to make sure he behaved.

Once the king sat down and we took our seats, Mr. Advisor began to state the case against Themi. I hadn't realized that he would be present and there to challenge Themi.

"Your Highness, Themi, your niece, has created a chaotic mess. She has been disrespectful of your family and the rules and should remain under house arrest for five years." Five years? Cruel and bizarre.

Themi shot up from her seat. "Your Highness, with respect, your advisor is wrong, as are the rules. I was—"

Mr. Advisor interrupted her rudely. "She is wrong. She has brought unnecessary attention to the kingdom and the royal family and must be silenced."

"Father," Bodhi intervened, "you promised me that you would at least listen to Themi and Maddie. They are trying to help make the kingdom a better place. Themi is trying to help the image of our family, not hurt it. It's not like some of the others in our family, like my younger sister Hassa, and the mess she made last month." Turning to me and the rest of our group, he elaborated, "My sister, Hassa, acts very spoiled, and last month when she was visiting Newtown, she got mad at some dude who was fixing the chandelier in her apartment. He almost broke one of her vases when he slipped on his ladder and she screamed at him, telling him he was useless. And then she told her bodyguard that the guy should die."

I heard myself say, "That's seriously messed up. Normal people don't go around saying someone should be killed for breaking a vase, or *almost* breaking a vase."

Bodhi said, "Yeah, I know. But that's my spoiled little sister. Luckily, the guards had more sense than my sister. They convinced her to let him apologize, and she made the guy kiss her feet. The press had a field day with a leaked photo of it."

"Bodhi, enough," said the king. "Your sister is just young and silly. And she's just a girl."

Oh, no, you didn't. You did not just dismiss all girls again. I felt Aunt AK squeeze my right shoulder, probably to encourage me to stay calm. But it was too late. Five days in the kingdom and I had lost patience. I stood up. "Uh, hello? I'm a girl, she's a girl, she's a girl, and her and her and her." I pointed to all the girls and women around me. Everyone gasped at my audacity to challenge the king so directly, but I continued.

"I'm tired of everyone in this place treating us like we're stupid second-class citizens just because we're girls. We are just as capable and as smart as boys. And if your daughter is not kind or fair, it's because she's not nice, not because she's a girl."

"My dad spoiled her," Bodhi added. "She may be my sister, Dad, but she's not nice or kind, you have to admit that. Stop defending bad behavior from her and the other royals."

"Bodhi! She's your sister. Where is your sense of honor?" The king's voice was becoming more agitated. "We don't speak ill about our family in front of others." Protocol was more important to the king than anything else.

"Dad, that's what you always say. Can't you see that everyone is talking about how badly behaved Hassa and the royals are? Just because they don't say it to our faces doesn't mean that they don't think it. It took Themi and Maddie here to make us even talk about the FP and the harsh rules about driving and wearing tents. You don't ever want to talk about anything. You just want me to obey. Obey you. Obey the family honor. I can't. I can't do it anymore!" Bodhi was having a complete meltdown. It was not what I had planned on, but I was grateful for the turn of events.

"I care too much for my kingdom," Bodhi continued, emotion choking his voice. "I care too much for the well-being of my people."

After a long pause, the king sighed. Bodhi's words had pierced through his tough exterior. "I think, my son, that maybe you have a point. Seems maybe you are thinking more like a king than me." Looking only at Bodhi, he softly said, "I have been so busy protecting the role of being the king that I have forgotten that I need to act like a king and take care of the people. And you," the king said, his voice thick with tender pride for his favorite son, "you, Bodhi, I think you have your grandfather's courage."

"I'm just like you were, Father, when you were my age."

"Maybe, my son. Age may give a person experience and wisdom, although not always, but life can wear you down and make you timid, too. Bruised by life, many of us, perhaps me included, become too cautious and frankly too fearful of the FP. Whereas you, my son, you still have the fearless courage of youth and the belief that change can happen."

"Tradition can be good, Father, but only if it's for everyone's benefit, not just for half the people—men, rich folks, or whatever. I mean, seriously, we know stuff that we didn't know five hundred years ago, like in science and medicine. Shouldn't how we treat people in the kingdom also show that we've evolved into kinder, more humane people?"

Prince Bodhi was saying everything I had been thinking since I came to the kingdom. Only he said it so much better. Themi was still standing, silently nodding in agreement. She understood that this was not just her quarrel with the king and the FP, but a debate between a father and his son.

The king said, "Well, you know the FP provides stability and rules for people to live by, which is essential for law and order."

"Yes, Your Highness, but what if the rules are unfair or wrong?" The words tumbled from my mouth without advance notice. Audible gasps surrounded me again. I looked at the faces of the king's advisors and Prince Bodhi. I looked at Alisha, Themi, and Sayara. All their faces were stunned. I knew commoners weren't supposed to question the king, but I wasn't intimidated by his royal status. To me, the king was really just Bodhi's dad. I was used to being able to debate with parents.

The king smiled, the kind of smile parents and adults give when they think a young person is clueless. "Maddie, you are young and do not fully understand the evils that can lurk in a country, in the kingdom. We need the faith and the FP to make sure that people are obedient and are not distracted by the evils in life."

"So, driving for women is an evil?" I questioned. More gasps. Had I crossed a line in questioning a king? Maybe, but if we didn't stand up for what we believed in, how could anything change? Besides, I was sure I was being polite. I turned to look at my dad, seated next to me. He wasn't shocked or mad. In fact, I think he almost looked happy—or was that pride? His supportive expression was enough to keep me going.

I continued. "Are girls evil? Why do you want us hidden from sight? Why can't we play soccer or work alongside the guys? We're just as smart."

"To the contrary, Maddie," the king's voice boomed with paternal authority. "We are protecting our women."

"From what?"

"From the evils of a sinful life!" The king was clearly getting a little agitated by my repeated questioning. It was one thing to debate his favorite son, Bodhi, and another to be questioned by pipsqueak me.

"By forbidding them from driving? By making them hide under ugly, black tents?" I was not accepting his pronouncements as any form of truth. It seemed like hogwash to me. Like someone had said these words to him and he was now just parroting them to me without really believing them himself.

"Our faith dictates it so," the king replied. "Something you would not understand."

Before I could respond, Themi intervened. "Actually, Uncle, no, our faith does not say that women can't drive or that they have to wear a tent and always cover their face. That's just how the FP in our kingdom has twisted it. All the faith says is that people should be conservative and modest, that's all. Men and women. There is nothing that says it has to be a law or a rule. There are lots of other kingdoms where people enjoy their faith without these unfair rules against girls."

Prince Bodhi added, "Dad, all people—women and men—can make their own choices about what to wear or whether they want to drive without the world coming to an end. Let people choose how they want to live their own lives, that's all. I have been trying to tell you this for years. The FP have abused the authority Grandfather gave them when he was dying. He may have foolishly trusted them, but they were just power-hungry and now they've taken advantage of our family's willingness to work with them. They are now in charge of the kingdom, not you, the king!"

Prince Bodhi's words seemed to suck the wind from the king's sails. His shoulders dropped, and his head shook slightly. "My son, you do not yet understand the dangers against you and our family if we challenge the FP. We have lost our way these past few decades. We got drunk on oil, and now the FP has become a monster. We have fed the beast, and now it is not so easy to tame it. Rules cannot be changed so easily, even bad rules."

This was an indirect admission that the FP's rules were wrong. I knew the king could make changes, but he lacked the courage.

"It's not fair," Prince Bodhi argued. "You and I both know, Dad, that everyone in our family goes outside the kingdom and totally does what they want. Mom and other women in our family choose what they want to wear and they drive. The guys do whatever they want as well, and some of it is stuff that's not so good anywhere. We've become a laughingstock, Dad. People know of this hypocrisy. How can anyone take us seriously when we say one thing officially, but then do whatever we want elsewhere? Even the grand master of the FP does whatever he wants when no one is looking."

Bodhi's words hit hard at the duplicity of the royals. I have hated duplicity my whole life. Maybe I hadn't experienced it so intensely as in the kingdom—but I always believe in consistency and living my life as I think and feel and not doing one thing and saying another.

It wasn't just the duplicity, though, it was about taking a stand and having an opinion. We owed it to one another to make sure the rules were fair for all of us, everywhere. Girls should not get any extra privileges just because they're girls, but they also shouldn't be penalized because they're girls, no matter where they happen to be born or live.

The king turned to my dad and said, "Our children want change, but my son does not have the wisdom of experience. Sometimes the real choice is between the lesser of two evils. These are not easy situations where simple solutions will make everyone happy."

My dad responded solemnly. "Perhaps, Your Highness, what Prince Bodhi may not have in experience, he makes up for in hope and optimism, however naïve it may seem to us. That's the power of the young—Prince Bodhi, Themi, Maddie, Sayara, and the others." I had never heard my dad speak so wisely and seriously. It was a new side to him, and I loved it.

"Perhaps," the king noted, "that is so, but the rules are still the rules. And change is not easy."

By this point, I was getting a little disheartened that the king kept saying he could not change the rules even though he agreed that they weren't fair. "I don't get it—if Your Highness understands that the rules are unfair against girls, why can't you just remove the ban and declare that women can now drive?"

"Maddie, I would like to," said the king, "but change has to come slowly, otherwise people may revolt."

"More likely the FP will revolt, Father," interjected Prince Bodhi, running his fingers through his hair in frustration.

"Yes, probably," said the king calmly. Turning to his son, he added, "Governing is a lot different than being an advocate, my son. You will understand that one day when you are king. You have to watch your enemies even closer than your supporters. The FP is just looking for a reason to toss our family out of power."

I understood what he said, but I didn't agree with it. I believed that if he just declared that he was ending some of the rules, most people would be happy, not mad. "Well, Your Highness," I hesitatingly began, "how about at least making the black tents optional? If girls want to wear them, they can, and if they don't, then they don't have to."

Themi quickly interjected, "In most countries, people choose to wear a dress or pants or whatever they want, but it's not required. They aren't jailed if they don't completely cover up under a tent."

The king paused, stroking his bearded chin. "Yes, Themi, I know it seems reasonable to you, but it can be hard to convince others. But making it an option, hmm," he said thoughtfully. "That might be doable. I like the option approach. Maybe we can do that with driving. Instead of ending a ban, we can say it more gently. Options, not enforced rules. Will people choose wisely?" he pondered. Turning to Mr. Advisor, the king asked, "How would it be if we gave women the choice to wear a tent or not? Gave them the option to drive if they want?"

My heart sank as I feared the worst coming from Mr. Throw-em-in-jail. The words burst from him like gunfire. "Terrible, terrible. Absolutely terrible. It would be chaos. Your Majesty, you cannot listen to these silly girls or to a young, inexperienced prince, even if he is your son. It's much more complicated, much more difficult. And besides, it's commanded by the FP."

Clearly he wasn't a guy who liked change.

I looked at the king's well-lined face to see how he would react. This time, there was something different on his face—determination. It made him look more like his son. At that moment, I realized that the king was finally deciding to do the right thing. Wasn't it Grammy who always said "Courage is doing what's right, not just following what has always been done or what others say"? Yep, he was about to do what kings are supposed to do—lead with kindness and reason. But instead of speaking, the king turned to his son.

Rising to the occasion and taking his dad's visual cue, Bodhi said gently, "Dad, what we really need in the kingdom is a new set of rules that better reflect who we are. Rules that encourage everyone to be kinder to each other."

Themi moved to stand next to her cousin, Prince Bodhi, forging their partnership in spirit, adding, "We really need laws that treat everyone as equal and valued, regardless of whether they are rich or poor, native or foreign, royal or not royal, male or female. Rules that allow everyone to have an opinion and to respectfully debate and disagree. The FP can't just decide whatever they want, whenever they want. They can't abuse the faith just to keep power and control. People are wondering why we royals do not protect the rights of people against the FP. The time has come to end the FP. We don't need them anymore."

"Outrageous!" screamed Mr. Advisor. "You will lose your power and your throne. You will be banished. The FP will revolt! Your Majesty, you cannot listen to a young boy, even if he is your son. And your niece, just a girl. I beg of you, come to your senses."

The king paused for just a moment, then told Mr. Advisor, "No, he is right. Themi is right. They are both right. The time for change has come." The king stood up and stretched out his arms. "And with that, since you cannot accept the changing times, it is time for you to retire. Please go now." He dismissed Mr. Advisor with a wave of his hand. "Thank you for your service."

It was so sudden, none of us expected this twist, least of all Mr. Advisor.

Mr. Advisor was ready to pounce and fight back, but hesitated. He looked around, registering that he was outnumbered in bodies and in spirit. But he was not done. You could see that in his glassy, beady eyes—the determination to retaliate later, when the moment was right. He bowed gracefully if not honorably. "I serve at your pleasure. I will take your leave." He slithered backward until he reached the door. Then he turned and walked out, slamming the door behind him.

"Another enemy. Father, I am sorry."

The king surprised us with his response. "Pay him no attention. Bodhi, one day in the future when you are king, you will have worse enemies. That's the nature of this job."

"Uncle," Themi solemnly said, "if you make the changes letting women drive and choose what they want to wear, among other things, you will be remembered as a very courageous king."

"Themi," the king said, looking at her gently, "I know that you are frustrated with me, as your uncle and as your king. We have not spent any time together, and I do not know anything about what girls like you want to achieve in the kingdom. But that has been my mistake. I have not listened or tried to understand your perspective. I see now that you along with my son are the future of our country. You can help guide the way."

It wasn't clear when the driving ban was going to be lifted, but at that moment, with the king, Bodhi, and Themi in agreement about actually making changes soon, we had hope.

We left the king's great chamber together. All of us—Themi, Hariz, Prince Bodhi, Sayara, Alisha, and me—walked out with our arms linked together. I knew that with my friends, new and old, together we'd change the world, one unfair rule at a time.

Acknowledgments

I would like to clearly note that this is a work of fiction. Any similarities to real people, events, or places are purely coincidental. Although, in reality, this story could happen in more places than you might initially think.

I am indebted to countless people from around the world, who over the years have shared their experiences, perspectives, opinions, and insight—collectively enabling me to create this tale. Thank you to you all.

In the final steps of writing and editing, I was fortunate to have insightful comments from my early young readers, Katie, Anoushka, Sarina, and Catherine. My gratitude to Holly for carefully editing while helping me make sure that Maddie's, Sayara's, and the rest of the cast's voices stayed true to their characters.

To my global family of choice, my enduring gratitude for your kind friendship and love.

To my parents, Vaiju and Prafulla, for living incredibly useful, generous, kind, and thoughtful lives—leading by their own example.

To my boys—Shanth, Yash, and Anand—who make the sun shine in my world each and every day. Their very essence reminds me to find the balanced middle way in life.

To all my readers, thank you for joining Maddie and Sayara on their first adventure. I hope that this story touches a part of your heart, soul, and life.

Curious about Maddie and Sayara's next adventure?
Explore www.maddieandsayara.com.

About the Author

S anjyot considers herself young in spirit. She believes that we're all equal regardless of gender, race, religion, or any other personal characteristics. She believes that no matter where you live, everyone should have *equality of opportunity*, although not necessarily equality of outcomes. She works in a number of ways to help people understand more about different people, other cultures, and the world at large. She's lived in many places and considers herself a curious resident of planet Earth.

She hopes to hear from you.
www.maddieandsayara.com

CPSIA information can be obtained
at www.ICGtesting.com
Printed in the USA
LVOW12s0359101117
555721LV00001B/177/P